EVEN STRENGTH

A SAINTS AND SINNERS / AVIATORS HOCKEY
CROSSOVER NOVEL

SOPHIA HENRY

KRASIVO CREATIVE

EVEN STRENGTH

ISBN: 978-1-949786-45-3

Cover Design: Amanda Shepard, Shepard Originals
Editing by: Kelly Bahney, The Literary Brew
Proofreading by: Julie Delva

"We must be willing to let go of the life we planned so as to have the life that is waiting for us."
~ Joseph Campbell

#BeKindLoveHard

* * *

CONNECT with Sophia:
SophiaHenry.com

PATREON
INSTAGRAM
AMAZON
BOOKBUB

PROLOGUE

VANYA

I haven't done many outlandish things in my life, but making the decision to defect from the USSR to join the Detroit Chargers NHL team might go down as the craziest thing I'll ever do.

Time will tell.

Although the plan to have me sneak away from my team, the Central Scarlet Army, at the World Ice Hockey Championships has been months in the making, it still makes my stomach spin and my head swirl. I know what I have to do, but actually doing it is going to be the biggest test of my life.

We all thought getting away from the team without anyone noticing was going to be one of the most challenging parts—and it was, but now that I'm standing inside a hotel with my agent, a friend who's translating and helping me defect, and two members of the Chargers organization, I realize there are so many other moving pieces.

Once I make it to America, I should be fine, but if anything goes wrong from now until the plane from Stockholm to New York takes off, I'm as good as dead.

Kirya and I are huddled in the lobby of the hotel, down the road from where the teams playing in the World Ice Hockey Championship have been staying over the last two weeks with two representatives from the Chargers.

The tournament is over.

The USSR won.

They don't know they're about to lose.

Chris Brookins, the Chargers Assistant General Manager, asks something in English, peering at Kirya with round, wire-rimmed glasses. The tall, thick man was known as an enforcer when he played in the seventies. Although he seems like he can hold his own, he's smart to be wary. They must really want me because the fact the Chargers are working with federal agencies to help me defect surprises the shit out of me. All these years, I thought they were scared of the big bad Russians.

If we get caught, we'll all get into major trouble. The Americans could be jailed, but Kirya and I would get a one-way ticket to the firing squad.

"Kirill Antonov, his agent and translator. I'm the one who's been communicating with your reporter friend," he answers in confident English. He translates for me quickly, which I appreciate.

When they talk over my head, I feel like I don't know what's going on, and since I'm the one who's got the most on the line if this plan falls apart, I need to be informed of every conversation, no matter how trivial.

Brookins glances at me for confirmation, and I nod. I'd trust Kirya even if he didn't translate for me. We've known each other for so long, I consider him a brother.

After they'd drafted me last June, the Chargers had to find a way to contact me, knowing the State would never let an organization offering money and freedom anywhere near their athletes. They asked a reporter from their local newspaper who learned Russian during his years in the military to meet with me while he was in Alaska covering another international hockey tournament.

Under the guise of writing a story about the Central Scarlet Army team, the reporter was allowed access to me for an interview. Before he left, he presented me with a Chargers magazine, telling me that it would give me some information about the team. Inside was a letter from the Chargers, letting me know they'd selected me in the NHL Entry Draft, and they would do everything in their ability to bring me over whenever I was ready to come to America.

But the letter was in English, so I couldn't read it. Even without an understanding of the contents, I knew enough not to share it with my supe-

riors. Since Kirya and I have been friends our entire lives and I knew he spoke English, I took it to him to translate.

Although we hadn't seen each other much since taking different paths in life as teenagers, when I called asking to meet him, Kirya's only questions were: when and where?

At our meeting, I told him I came to him because he was the only person I trusted that spoke English and would be excited to engage in something illegal and dangerous.

How could he say no?

Once Kirya translated what the letter from Detroit said, I agreed to leave the USSR without hesitation. My old friend seemed surprised. I guess he thought I would blindly follow the Russian machine my entire life.

But he couldn't be more wrong. I'd been hoping for an opportunity like this. You can't travel the world and see how other people live and not be envious. I love Russia, but I've already won a gold medal and multiple World Championship titles. I've accomplished everything I could playing for my country—I want more.

Kirya and I discussed what defection would mean for me as an army officer. If I were caught, I would be considered a traitor, a criminal. A light sentence would be spending the rest of my life at a labor camp in Siberia. Most likely, I'd be killed as soon as I got back into the country.

If there's one thing about being a product of the Russian hockey system that serves me well, it's confidence. Failing is not an option. To me, there are no consequences to leaving, only rewards. I've seen the older guys on the team fight for too much to let the opportunity slide. I don't have the same mental investment in the Soviet system as they do because I grew up among political turbulence.

Athletes will always bring money—we can be bought, sold, and marketed to bring in revenue. Why would I do that in the Soviet Union where the corrupt state sports department would take the majority of the money and leave me poor? At least in the NHL, I have the opportunity to rack up millions of dollars in my bank account.

It was at the first meeting that I asked Kirya if he would contact Detroit to help him with the process, and he agreed. Since then, he and the reporter have been in communication, acting as translators for our respective parties, making plans to get me to Detroit.

My life is in the hands of a Russian mobster.

The bustling lobby has my jaw and shoulders tense. I'm aware of every person that passes. The team never travels out of the country without Sovietsport officials and KGB agents. There are checks and balances to keep each athlete in line and accounted for. Once someone realizes I'm not in my room, there will be a manhunt. All hands on deck, searching for their missing superstar.

Although it was the Detroit organization's idea to steal me away during the tournament, I can guarantee Kirya has the most experience with shady situations out of the four of us standing here. The suits from the Chargers think he's my agent and translator, which is fine with me. They'd shit their designer pants if they knew about half of the things Kirya's done. Hell, I'm sure I would too.

Next to me, Kirya stiffens. The hair rises on the back of my neck, alerting me that there might be a problem.

"We need to move this. I think we were followed," he tells me before translating for the men.

"Fuck," Brookins hisses an English word I'm familiar with, glancing at Jack Owens, a senior scout with the Detroit organization.

Sweat glistens above his eyebrows. He's nervous—understandably so. The Chargers have spent too much money and put their asses on the line for me to get caught.

I understand enough about the male ego to assume that when they agreed to do this, they probably had some romantic notion that it would be fun, like playing spies in a Hollywood movie. The reality of helping someone defect is a lot less glamorous.

These two American men must be courageous or stupid because what they are doing is against the law. They may think they're stealthy, but this will be all over the news in every country. And they're fucking with the Soviet government—the ultimate enemy. Maybe this is the final phase of the Cold War. Steal one of the Soviet Union's most prized possessions and watch the country crumble.

Money trumps everything—even politics. Detroit wants their draft pick and they'll do whatever it takes to get me, even if they have to bend international rules to steal me from another country.

Kirya jumps into action. "There is a mall at Hamngatan and Regeringsgatan called the Gallerian. When you get there, drive around to the back entrance on Jakobsgatan. We will meet you out there," he says.

We all know KGB would be looking for me as soon as the CSA coaches and trainers realized I wasn't in my room. I'm relieved he's able to think quickly under this kind of pressure because I'm not in the right mental state to figure anything out. Thankfully, he told me I didn't have to. All I have to do is follow him and do what he tells me to do.

"Perfect. We'll be there in twenty minutes." The men walk away quickly, finally comprehending that time is of the essence in a situation like this. Suddenly, Chris turns around and asks, "Is he certain he wants to do this? To come with us?"

"One hundred percent," Kirya answers without asking me. He translates and hands me a small backpack as we walk, exiting the hotel through a different door to avoid being seen leaving with the Americans.

"I brought you extra clothes and a toothbrush, toothpaste, stuff like that," he says. "There's enough to get you to America. Once you're there, someone from the team will take you shopping."

I thank him as I take the bag. Because I needed everything to seem normal, I left my room with only a few personal things and documents I could fit in my pockets.

On the street, we hail a cab, and Kirya directs the driver to the Gallerian.

My stomach is torn up like New Year's Day after a long night celebrating with champagne and vodka. Only today, it feels like I could vomit at any moment. I know Kirya is worried about me because he keeps glancing my way. His fingers tap on his thigh, as if counting how long he'll stay silent before confronting me. I assume it won't be long since he's never been one to keep his mouth shut.

"Are you rethinking the decision?" Kirya asks.

"No." A thick patch of hair flops over my right eye as I shake my head. I'm surprised he can't read my mind since we've shared the responsibility of protecting Stasya for as long as I can remember.

It's not that my sister is weak. On the contrary, she's one of the strongest women I know. But even the strongest people need help when they're forced to live with our father, a raging drunk who uses his daughter as his personal punching bag ever since Mama died. When I'm home, he's in a fairly good mood because we're discussing my games and success. But when I'm gone, she gets the brunt of his depression.

"Then what are you thinking about?" He hits my thigh with the back of his hand. "Your brain is working so hard, you have steam coming from your ears."

I chew on my bottom lip for a few seconds, trying to figure out how to bring up Stasya. I feel like a horrible human being for leaving her behind. But Kirya, out of all people, understands you do what you have to do for the greater good, no matter who might get hurt.

Stasya won't understand right now, but defecting puts me on the path to a better life. After a few years, when I'm established, I'll get her here, too. She's strong and resilient. She's lived life without me before, and she'll do it again.

Though I'm confident in my decision, I'm still filled with fear and uncertainty about defecting. It goes against the Soviet propaganda we've been brainwashed with our entire lives. Especially someone like me, an officer in the Scarlet Army and a player on the most successful hockey team of all time. Living in that environment for so long makes the weight of my decision heavier because the costs of leaving are higher for me.

"I'm worried about Stasya," I finally say.

Kirya's head snaps to me. I know he's fond of Stasya, probably more so than he is of me.

I push the hair out of my eyes only for it to fall right back. "Investigators will think she knew about what I was planning, Kirya. They'll question her—harass her. We're too close. They won't believe that she didn't know."

The KGB will interrogate my entire family, but they'll focus on Stasya because of our relationship. Even though she truly didn't know, they won't stop until they break her.

Our eyes lock. "Stasya will be fine," he assures me.

As I nod, my shoulders relax in relief. Then I turn my head to look out the window and stare at the bustling streets of Stockholm. All those people going on with their normal lives.

The cab drops us off at the front of the mall on Hamngatan. We wander around for a little while, going in and out of a few stores, giving the perception we're just two guys shopping as we make our way to the doors near the back. Paranoia seeps into every thought. If we were being watched at the hotel, we're definitely being followed.

"It's been over twenty minutes. We need to get to the back door and see if the car is here," Kirya whispers.

"Okay," I agree. My hand shakes as I place a button-down dress shirt back onto a rack. A hardened criminal like Kirya probably thinks I don't have the balls to pull this off. Despite my nerves, I have more determination to do this than I ever have before.

When he punches my shoulder, I lock eyes with him. "You can do this."

I nod and give him two thumbs up. It's probably not very reassuring, but I'm not a pussy. I made this decision months ago and I'm not turning back or jeopardizing it now. Being nervous is a normal reaction for anyone in this situation.

Out of the corner of my eye, I see two large men in shabby, gray trench coats and sunglasses coming toward us. Kirya sees them too, and he's one step ahead of me.

"Follow me," he barks out the command. "Fast!"

We flee from the store quickly, winding through as many different racks as we can to try to lose the men in pursuit.

As soon as we're out of the store, I see the large, double doors that lead to the back exit and bolt toward them. I don't need Kirya to tell me to run as fast as I can. I just hope he can keep up. Thankfully, when I push the door open, he's at my heels.

As soon as we're outside, I point to Brookins standing next to a navy-blue car with the engine still running. The American is as white as a ghost as if the impact of the situation is just hitting him.

When he sees us, he wastes no time opening the back door and ushering us in before getting in himself. The driver hits the gas before he closes the door.

"Do you think we're being followed?" Owens asks as we drive through the streets of Stockholm.

"Absolutely," Kirya answers.

I didn't think it was possible for either of the Americans' faces to lose any more color, but they drain a shade lighter before my eyes. There's no reason for Kirya to sugarcoat the situation. We won't be completely safe until the plane to New York is off the ground.

Brookins turns around and addresses me. "You can still go back if you want. This is your last chance to change your mind."

I know I'm entering the point of no return.

Before Kirya can finish translating, I interject, "No. I go."

When we get to the U.S. Embassy, Kirya and I have to sneak inside wearing clothes borrowed from the Americans. The less we look like ourselves, the better because embassies are always being watched.

Once we've made it inside, a sense of relief washes over me even though I know we're not in the clear yet.

Kirya pulls the tattered, gray Boston College sweatshirt Brookins gave him to wear over his head and tosses it onto the small coffee table next to him.

I hover halfway between the door and the small office Brookins and Owens slipped into as soon as we arrived. We've made it one step further, but we're still not in the clear. KGB or Sovietsport agents could be outside for all we know.

Kirya sits in one of the uncomfortable office chairs, sipping black coffee and listening as Brookins and Owens organize paperwork. Some of it, like my NHL contract, is already here at the Embassy because Detroit's owner had faxed it over previously. But the travel documents saying I signed it would need to be drawn up today with both me and the Detroit representatives.

A TV blares from the next room. I don't know Swedish, but I can clearly make out my name and "USSR hockey." My disappearance being all over the Swedish news already doesn't bode well for us.

My knees shake as more minutes tick by. I've never known or researched anyone who defected so I'm no expert; but I understand enough about Soviet Union officials and the KGB to know time is of the essence. The longer we're in Sweden, the less likely I'll make it to North America.

While the Detroit representatives and the embassy agents work diligently on the documents, I get permission to call my family.

I hesitate before dialing the number. This call could be a death sentence for my family. I take a deep breath and let it out audibly before dialing the number. When an operator answers, I don't think anything of it. I assume the Embassy has someone directing all outbound calls. I ask the operator to connect me to Stasya.

Kirya stare is intense as he watches me. His Adam's apple bobs as he swallows thickly.

I put my hand over the mouthpiece and say, "They put me on hold."

His eyebrows veer together as if he's noticed something odd, which makes my blood run cold. Then, a different operator comes on the line and asks me who I am and why I want to get in touch with Anastasiya Kravtsova.

"Fuck," I spit and slam the receiver on the base.

"What happened?" Kirya asks, jumping from his chair.

"It wasn't the same operator. It was someone asking questions," I say gravely. "I think they know where we are. They are listening to calls."

"No more names," Brookins snaps. "If you make a phone call, we don't use names, got it?"

When Kirya translates, I nod.

"Excuse me," he says to stop a passing woman. He points at the television screen. "What are they saying on TV?"

"They're searching for a player from the Russian National Team. They say he's been kidnapped."

His voice is less confident when he translates. He's been stable and secure through every step of this process. For the first time he seems rattled.

And for the first time, it crosses my mind, that I may never make it to America.

* * *

For as much drama as it was from the hotel to the Embassy, the drive from the Embassy to the airport is uneventful. Still, all four of us are on high alert because we know there's plenty of time for something to go wrong.

Kirya and I walk around the airport in our ill-fitting, borrowed clothes until it's time to board. We don't want to sit in one place for too long, and we definitely don't want to be seen with the guys from the Chargers.

Over the course of my life, I've been in some intense situations—broken up fights before my drunk father can hurt my sister, final seconds of a game we needed to win, getting broken down by a sadistic coach—but I've never breathed such a huge sigh of relief as I do when the airplane leaves the ground.

Kirya turns to me and smiles broadly. "Ivan Kravtsov, Lieutenant in the Scarlet Army, you are officially a criminal—a traitor of the highest level. Is there anything you'd like to say?"

I breathe a sigh of relief and glance at my white knuckles, realizing I've been squeezing the arms of the chair like a first-time flyer.

"Where's that stewardess? I need a drink."

* * *

As soon as we step inside the terminal at JFK International Airport in New York City, reporters swarm us. Despite knowing I'm safe right now, my heart still threatens to burst from my chest. My defection and arrival in New York are all over the news. But here, I'm untouchable.

I slip sunglasses on and pull the baseball cap over my eyes, trying to keep my identity concealed despite feeling like one of those asshole KGB agents I made fun of in Stockholm.

Kirya's job is done. I'm officially on U.S. soil with all the paperwork I'll need in Detroit for now. If anything else comes up, the Chargers will take care of it.

This is where we part ways. The Americans and I will drive to Detroit from here, and my friend goes on with whatever business he has to tend to here. As much as I'd love if he could stay with me and be my full-time translator, I know he can't. The Chargers already have me set up with Viktor Berezin, a professor who teaches Russian at Michigan University and translates on the side. It's probably better to be seen with a teacher than a high-ranking soldier in the bratva.

"Thank you," Chris Brookins tells Kirya, still speaking as they shake hands. I don't know what else he says, but I know enough English to make out the words for spasibo. *I studied how to say the absolute basics—greetings, manners, a few pleasantries, yes and no. Though, I can understand a bit more until the conversation starts going too fast. Then I'm lost again.*

Kirya grins broadly. "Always happy to help a comrade escape the regime."

After shaking hands with Owens, he turns to me. "I'll be checking in with you soon, but if you need anything, don't hesitate to call."

"Thank you," I say. "For everything."

"It's my pleasure to help, my friend." When I bring him in for a hug, he slaps my back. "We will meet again."

Before I let him go, I whisper, "I have a lump in my stomach, Kirya. Promise me you'll take care of Stasya."

"Don't worry. I always have and I always will," he gives me his word as he backs away.

1

VANYA

The doorbell rings for the umpteenth time. I heard it the first and second time, and several times after that, but ignored them all.

Every time I hear that bell, the hair on the back of my neck rises and my brain kicks into flight mode.

I'm afraid it's the KGB.

Then I laugh to myself because the KGB wouldn't ring. They'd break down the fucking door.

A quick glance out my bedroom window, which faces the street, tells me it's the guy delivering my suit. After being ignored for so long, you'd think he'd leave it. But people in America are persistent.

Like the KGB.

Part of me hoped he would assume I wasn't home and leave. It would give me the perfect excuse to miss the event tonight.

He doesn't leave, though. That persistent guy just keeps ringing the damn doorbell until I give in.

"Coming!" I yell as I bound down the staircase. Before he arrived, I'd been lying on my bed, feeling sorry for myself and moping about life in America.

Imagine the nerve—moping about freedom—the one thing I've

wanted since I was old enough to realize I'd been living under oppression my entire life.

"For a minute there, I almost thought you weren't home," the man says with a smile, holding a nylon bag from his fingertips.

"Yes?" I ask, watching him shifting from foot to foot restlessly. I can make out a few words, but overall, I have no clue what he said.

"Here's your suit, Sir. Cleaned and pressed." He hands me the bag. "The shop has communicated the price to you, I believe?"

"*Spasibo*," I thank him, hoping it's a good enough answer because I still don't know what he's saying.

I collect the suit with one hand while digging the other into the pocket of my shorts to hand him some cash. Then I shut the door without waiting for change or his reply.

"I—Sir!" I hear him call from the other side of the door.

With an agitated sigh, I open it again. "Is good, yes?"

"It's w-way too much," he stutters, flipping through the cash as if counting it again to be sure. He plucks out a twenty and hands it back to me.

I just shrug and say, "Is good," before shutting the door again.

I drape the suit over the back of the couch and exhale loudly as I plop down beside it. I check the oversized clock on the wall above the television. It's just a few minutes past five p.m., and despite the fact that the party won't start for another two hours, it feels like it's only a few minutes away.

Though this is usually one of my favorite events of the year, I don't feel like going tonight. I'm homesick, exhausted, and I don't feel like pretending I can understand the conversations going around me in English.

When I got to America, my main focus was to be able to communicate with my teammates and coaches. I'm here to play hockey, after all. I can understand some small talk, but I usually just nod and hope my expression doesn't look as blank as my head feels when I'm surrounded by English.

The team set me up with a translator, so I didn't put a huge amount of time into learning the language. My understanding skills have gotten much better, but learning more than what's necessary hasn't been a priority.

I've taken a lot of flak in the media for it. Not that I can read it—or care—but my agent does. Kirill, Kirya to those close to him, wanted me to learn English quickly and play nice so I could be a media "darling" as he calls it. He wants half of the people in the arena at Chargers games wearing a "Kravtsov" jersey. Media and fan appreciation, combined with my skills and how integral I am to the team's success, means bigger contracts and endorsements—a win for both of us.

Kirya is a very smart, crafty man. That's why I went to him first when the Chargers organization slipped me a message in a media program. Kirya told me the note said they'd drafted me. They took a huge chance "wasting" a draft pick on me because Russian players weren't allowed to go to America then. Not without the Central Scarlet Army's permission. And agreeing to let them take more than half of my contract just to go wasn't something I'd ever agree to.

Not that the CSA would ever let *me* go. They weren't interested in giving up their young, talented players. They only allowed old guys past their prime and at the end of their career to go to America.

The memory of the night we escaped still haunts my dreams. Although I've been here for a few years now, I remember it like it was yesterday. I'd never had such a mix of emotions. Fear, disbelief, and finally relief.

Well, there was relief for a brief moment—until the weight of what I'd done to my twin sister hit me. Despite living my dream—and making more money than I ever thought possible—guilt and grief overshadowed relief and joy.

I promised Stasya I'd take her to American with me if I ever got the chance. I promised I'd remove her from a life of abuse in Russia. But when we talked about those plans, I'd assumed I'd get to American legally, with the Central Scarlet Army's permission.

Involving her in an intense plot to defect that was concocted by the mafia was not something I was going to do.

I rake my hands through my hair, willing myself to stop thinking about it. The defection, Russia, my betrayal.

Stasya's been here for years. She's safe and successful—having opened her own clothing store in New York City. We've discussed the situation at length, and she forgave me once she understood my reasons.

Yet, I can't leave the past behind. Despite having an amazing life here in America, I still feel homesick—like I'm missing something.

I lay lazily on the couch for a few more minutes before standing up. The event is more of a "team function" than a party, and I've already scheduled a car to be here at 6:30 p.m. to pick me up.

Plus, I know I'll have a good time once I get there. I can always have fun at a party.

I sigh and lift myself off the couch. Guess I better shower and get ready.

* * *

BY THE TIME the Town Car pulls up at the Roostertail, a stylish and sophisticated social space on the Detroit River, my foul mood from earlier has been replaced with excitement about the event. It's a fundraiser for the local children's hospital where some of my teammates and I volunteer every month. I love visiting the kids—taking photos, signing autographs.

Some of the guys get to read them stories, but I'm not at a point with my English where I can read a book, not even a children's book. Actually, maybe I should bring a picture book for the toddlers, it might be a good learning experience for both me and them.

This event is for Chargers season ticket holders. They get to mix and mingle with players and other special guests. All the money goes to the hospital.

When I arrive, it's still cocktail hour. Later, there will be a DJ and people on the dance floor, but right now, there's an older guy hunched over the piano, fingers dancing across the keys. Guests mull around, chatting happily, snapping photos, and sipping their drinks.

"Ivan! You made it. How are you enjoying the party?" Brookins appears from nowhere, dressed in a dark blue Italian suit and holding an almost-empty glass of wine. Our GM looks the same as he does any other day. The only exception is that his hair is styled a bit differently.

"I wish Viktor is here," I tell him honestly. My interpreter, Viktor Berezin, is only around after games to help me talk to the press or during events when I need to interact for team business purposes. I'm on my own for fundraiser mixers with fans.

"He's a beauty, right?"

"Yes, s—" I haven't even finished forming the words when he speaks again.

"Wait, you don't have a drink? Where's a waiter when you need one?" He looks around and whistles at one of the several people carrying trays of drinks. "Here you go." He hands me a glass and points to the largest crowd in the room. "That's where you need to be."

When I look again, the majority of my teammates are in that group, and fans are gathered around. Flashbulbs go off every few seconds, creating flickers of light in the dim room. I take a sip of the wine and head toward the group.

"There's our favorite Russian left wing!" Erik Simmons, Chargers captain, greets me as I approach, alerting everyone around that I've arrived.

"I am here," I say, holding my arms out and flashing a smile at the fans.

Within seconds, I'm mobbed with hugs, handshakes, and photo requests. Over the next hour and a half, I'm having a blast interacting best I can with the partygoers and my teammates, who help rescue me from the questions I can't understand.

The Chargers fans are really cool and respectful. No one pressures me or expects more than I can give. They're actually extremely forgiving. It's like they understand that I only know so much English and go out of their way to make me feel comfortable.

Though I'm enjoying myself, I need a break before I can take another flash blinding my eyes. I excuse myself quickly and move across the room toward the wall of floor to ceiling windows.

The Roostertail has a huge patio and a gorgeous view of the skyline. I missed the sunset over the river, but I can still take in the sight of the lights twinkling off the water. I drop my wine glass on a table and step outside.

The atmosphere outside is much different. I can still hear the faint sound of the piano, a quiet, soothing melody. The night breeze seems chillier than usual, and it smells like it's going to rain. I lean my arms against the rail and take a deep breath, looking across the river at Canada on the other side.

Suddenly, the peace and quiet is interrupted by a woman's voice saying something in English.

"No English," I say, glancing over my shoulder.

Standing at the door is a woman with the most beautiful set of bright, blue eyes I've ever seen. She's got long blonde hair, rosy cheeks, and an infectious smile. I'd recognize her anywhere, but I must be wrong because there's no way the woman I'm thinking of would be here tonight.

When she moves closer, I see her face properly and realize it *is* her.

Ekaterina Novikova, Russian tennis phenom. She'd taken the sports world by storm when she won a Grand Slam last year at only fifteen. Tennis is my favorite sport to watch, and her career has been exciting to follow since she broke onto the scene. A comrade who's doing so well in her sport is always something to pay attention to.

Not to mention, she's absolutely gorgeous—as evidenced by her face gracing every magazine cover from Sports Illustrated to Cosmopolitan over the last year.

"No English? Russian maybe?" she asks in our native tongue. "Are you Ivan Kravtsov?" Her thick, perfectly-shaped eyebrows veer together as if she's trying to figure out if she's got the right person.

"In the flesh," I answer, grinning. "What is a beautiful, Russian tennis champion doing at a random party in Detroit?" I ask, taking her shoulders in my hands, and kissing her cheeks three times, as is custom.

Her tan skin flushes pink at the apples of her cheeks. "I'm one of the special guests." She uses her fingers as quotes when she says 'special guests.'

I'd been so busy with the team and fans, I didn't even look around the rest of the party. Usually, the special guests are athletes from other Detroit sports teams. Nice enough people, but I wouldn't recognize them from any of the paying attendants.

"I've been looking all over for you," she says.

"You've been looking for me?" I ask, puzzled. "Why is that?"

"It's not every day that I'm at a party with someone I can talk to in Russian. Translating English all the time can be so exhausting." She waves toward the door, then rubs her temples.

"You're very good with the language. I've seen enough of your interviews to know that." I laugh.

"You've seen many of my interviews?" she asks, tilting her head down and giving me a coy smile. She flips her hair over her shoulder then turns to rest her elbows on the railing. "Are you interested in me, Vanya?"

I watch as she looks out at the river. "I'm always interested in a talented comrade who made it out."

"So am I."

"Yes, Zhenya told me," I say, mentioning the name of my former teammate who came to America a year after I did. Last I heard, he and Katya were seeing each other.

She turns to me and pushes my chest lightly. "Oh! You boys were sharing locker room stories, yes?"

I shake my head innocently and meet her teasing eyes. "Never."

"Zhenya is a wonderful man, but we're not together."

"I'm sorry to hear that."

"You don't have to be. We both knew it wasn't going to work out, so we went our separate ways. He moved on, I moved on, and now everyone's happy," she says, shifting her body toward me as the words leave her lips. “Enough of my private life, though. How are you doing with everything here?”

“I could ask you the exact same question,” I reply.

She lets out a small laugh, then continues softly, “Your defection was international news, Vanya. I just want to make sure everything is okay for you here. Are you being harassed?”

“That’s quite a forward question, Katya,” I say, stiffening and backing away slightly. “For two people who just met.”

“I wasn’t trying to offend you.” She steps closer and places her hand on mine. “I’m genuinely concerned.”

My gaze moves from her hand on mine to her eyes. “I have no regrets about my decision.”

I may feel homesick sometimes, but I’m proud I made the decision to do what was best for my career and my life.

“Good. I know how difficult it must have been, but your bravery to go against the system paved the way for Russians, not just in sports, but all Russians.” She squeezes my hand. “I’ve never met a more courageous man, Vanya.”

“I—” I pause, searching for the words to say after such an amazing compliment. But I can’t think of anything, so I turn the tables on her. “Being in America looks good on you.”

“How so?” She tilts her head, eyes sparkling as she waits for my answer.

“You haven’t stopped smiling since we started speaking. I bet you didn’t smile like that back home.”

“Ahhh, you think my smile is an American influence?”

I nod. “Smiling all the time is very American. Have you ever met a Russian with a permanent grin?”

“Well, no, but that’s because there’s nothing to be permanently happy about over there.” She laughs, then adjusts her elbows on the railing. I catch the scent of baby powder mingling with vanilla. “Maybe I can’t stop smiling because I enjoy the company.”

Before I can respond to her compliment, one of the waiters comes out and addresses us. “Excuse me, Miss. You’re needed inside. Charlie requested you.”

"That's my coach. But you already know that from all the interviews you watch," she teases. "I'm sorry I have to go."

She stands straight, smooths imaginary wrinkles at the hips of her simple, yet elegant, cocktail dress, and flashes me that beautiful smile of hers one more time before following the waiter inside.

I'd gone out to have some alone time, and now that I'm finally by myself, I don't want to be alone anymore. The conversation with Katya was just starting to take off, and I don't want it to end.

I liked her already. I like the mix of confidence and innocence—the latter of which reminds me that she's only sixteen-years-old. Then again, winning major tennis championships at fifteen and ranking as second in the world a year later requires a lot of confidence and maturity.

After being so apprehensive about attending earlier, I'm glad I came. Though I've thoroughly enjoyed myself, meeting Katya has been the highlight of the night. Not only because she's beautiful and has the most gorgeous smile, but because we understand each other on so many levels. Like me, she's a foreigner in a strange, overwhelming land. As professional athletes, we live similar lives, and she understands the pressure and expectations.

The night breeze rustles through my hair, and I feel the first drops of rain. Time to get back inside and hang out with my teammates and fans. I fasten my suit coat and slip through the door before the sky lets loose.

"Where've you been, Doc?" Simmons asks when I rejoin my teammates. "We thought you left."

"I run into comrade out there," I nod toward the door to the patio.

After speaking with Katya, it feels as though a weight slipped off my shoulders. I spend the rest of the night laughing and talking with teammates and fans.

Every once in a while, I bring my glass to my lips and look through the crowd searching for the beautiful blonde who helped me feel at home for the first time since I arrived.

2

KATYA

NE YEAR LATER

TODAY'S TRAINING WAS GRUELING. Charlie hadn't worked me this hard since the qualifiers for Wimbledon last year. I've never shied away from the hard work it takes to win championships, but my coach is on a different kind of rampage today.

"We need to work on your serve. It needs to get harder and faster. It would be the most valuable advantage to your game," he'd said earlier this morning.

For the better part of five hours, all I've done is serve, serve, and serve some more.

"Again! Harder! Harder!"

I'm hitting the ball as hard and fast as I can, but I know he wants more. I've been working with Charlie since I was fourteen-years-old. He'll push me to go harder and faster until I'm so exhausted I can barely lift my arm.

"Good job, Champ. You did well today," he says, wrapping an arm across my shoulders and squeezing me into his chest. I smile and allow myself to enjoy the praise.

One of the best things about having Charlie as a coach is this. Despite the fact that he'd pushed me hard all day, he calls me champ and tells me I've done a good job.

I know some players on the circuit who have coaches from hell. There are people out there who think the best method to train athletes is to break them down completely to build them into a champion. I know that, not just from conversations with other players, but also because I had one of those coaches for years. Back in Moscow, the coach who taught me how to play wouldn't stop practice until he had me in tears.

Charlie has always been hard on me, but he takes my personality into consideration. He knows I shut down in that kind of environment. In fact, if my parents hadn't trusted my desire to become a professional player, I would have quit if I'd stayed with that coach. Instead, they talked to multiple tennis directors in countries all over the world and found Charlie. They even moved us to Florida so I could work with him.

I'd thought I'd gotten used to Charlie's unpredictable methods, but he never ceases to surprise me. Today was serving—which isn't that crazy—but last week he had me lifting weights with his fifty-pound English bulldog. He said I had to get out of the gym and do something fun. Let me tell you, holding a heavy, smelly, furry thing that wiggles and passes gas is not my idea of "fun." But once I got going, it actually was—except the passing gas part. And lifting a dog while doing squats felt just as good as doing it in the gym, Plus, I got some slobbery kisses as a reward.

No matter what crazy technique he tells me to do, I never argue, because I get results.

After an intense day of training, I sneak away to my favorite lunch place in Chicago. It's a cute, little diner-type place that has the best milkshakes. The retro décor looks authentic but it's bright and shiny like it's been updated recently.

The hostess recognizes me as a regular customer immediately

and leads me to my favorite spot, a booth in the front window. I love looking out at the hustle and bustle of downtown Chicago—any cold, busy city, really. It reminds me of home.

As much as I love my life in America and wouldn't change a thing about it, I miss Moscow. I miss the snow in the winter and the flowers in the summer. Sure, other places have both of those things, but there's something about home.

As I wait for my milkshake, I pull my first aid kit out of my duffle bag and tend to the blisters on my hand. I haven't had a blister in forever. If I would have realized I'd be doing an entire day of serving, I would've changed my grip before practice.

"You okay, honey?" The waitress asks as she sets a glorious vanilla milkshake in front of me.

"Yes. This is nothing." I wave my hand and give her an appreciative smile. "Thank you."

"Enjoy your shake."

Thankfully, I have a rest day from practice tomorrow. I don't think I've ever looked forward to a rest day the way I looked forward to this one. Instead of "rest," I have a photo shoot with Glonex, the company who makes the tennis rackets I use. I'm excited and nervous. I love modeling—maybe even more than I love tennis. But I'd never tell Charlie or my parents that.

"Hey."

I jump and almost spit out my shake when someone taps my shoulder.

I'm so engrossed in my thoughts I didn't even hear anyone come up behind me. When I turn, I see a familiar face. "Vanya? Hi!" I greet him, doing little to hide the excitement in my words. "What are you doing here?"

"We had a game last night," he replies, then points behind him. "This is the guys favorite lunch place."

There's a group of men gathered at a table in the back of the restaurant. A few are talking, but most have their heads down, eating their food. "What about you," he continues. "What are you doing in Chicago?"

"I'm training here this week because I have a shoot with Glonex tomorrow," I tell him with a proud grin. We only met a once, but I haven't stopped thinking about him since that day. And I can't keep the smile off my face now that I'm around him.

"A shoot?" he asks, then gestures to the booth. "Do you mind if I sit?"

"Y-yes, please," I kick myself for not thinking of offering him a seat before he had to ask.

Instead of taking a seat opposite me, as I expected, he slides in next to me. My heart flutters as I scoot over to give him more room.

"I have an endorsement with the company that makes my racket. We're shooting a commercial tomorrow."

"Katya! That's brilliant! Congratulations."

His praise makes my stomach swirl and warmth rush to my cheeks.

"So, how was the game?" I clear my throat and change the subject to take the attention off myself.

"It was close, but we won," he replies with a proud smile. "How's training going?"

"To be honest, I'm exhausted. I worked on serving for five hours straight and I feel like my arm could fall off at any minute."

He laughs. "Ah, yes. The grueling life of professional athletes."

"But we also get to splurge on milkshakes and not feel guilty about it, right?" I laugh.

"Is it that good?" he asks, pointing to the creamy heaven in a glass.

"Wait a minute, don't tell me you've never had a milkshake." My hands fly to my mouth in sheer surprise.

He laughs again and shrugs, his shoulder bumping mine. I love how we touch every time we move.

"You've lived in America for how long and you've never had a milkshake? It's one of the many pleasures of being in this lovely country." I gesture toward the window as if that encompasses the entirety of the United States.

"I haven't tasted all the pleasures I'd like yet, but I'm working on it." He gazes at me with an intensity that hints at much more than friendship. It makes me shiver from my head to my toes. I haven't felt like this about anyone before. Not even my last boyfriend, Zhenya. While, I liked him, I think it was the comfort of being with another Russian, especially when I was still new to America.

"Hey, V! We gotta get back to the bus before wheels up for the airport," one of his teammates calls from the back of the restaurant. The guys are standing up and throwing cash into a pile in the middle of the table.

He nods and holds up a finger, then turns back to me. "I'm sorry, but I have to go,"

He wants to spend more time with me, it's written all over his face. It reminds me of the last time we saw each other at that fundraiser in Detroit. We were just getting comfortable when Charlie called for me.

"It's okay. You don't have to apologize. The grueling life of professional athletes, right?" I wink.

"Exactly." He smiles and runs a hand through his dark blond hair. "It was wonderful to run into you again, Katya." He squeezes my knee before scooting out of the booth and standing to leave.

My smile disappears as soon as he and his teammates walk out the door. Just like that, I'm no longer interested in the milkshake in front of me, the one I hyped up so much. All I want is more time with Vanya.

Everything about him—his warm blue eyes, his wide smile, his unexpected touch—set fire to every nerve in my body. No one's ever made me feel this way before. But we both have careers that take us in different directions.

The kind of life I lead makes keeping real friends difficult—unless you count the other tennis players I'm always around. I get along with everyone just fine, but I don't want to hang out with only tennis players. I want to have friends who aren't competition. Friends who let me wind down and relax from the stress of the job instead of talking about it. The fact that Vanya appeared in my life, not once, but twice now, has to mean something.

"Hey."

I feel someone tap my shoulder again. When I turn around, Vanya's back.

"Did you forget something?" I ask, scanning the booth and table for something out of place.

"Yes." He touches my arm, jolting me out of my search. "But it's not anything physical."

I tilt my head toward him. "What does that mean?"

"I forgot to ask you for your number."

For a moment, I'm frozen, giddy with excitement. Then I remember what he asked for. "Oh!" I scramble through my duffle bag looking for something to write on. All I can find is a piece of gum. I pull it out slowly, then glance at Vanya.

He laughs and plucks it from my hand. Then he unravels the paper, pops it in his mouth, and hands the wrapper back to me. "Works for me."

Shaking my head, I scribble my mobile phone number on the paper. The phone is a huge, bulky thing, but it's a life saver for keeping in touch with all the travel I do.

When I give him the number, he says, "Talk to you soon, Sunshine." Then he winks and rushes out the door. I watch out the window as he jogs to catch up with his teammates.

The smile on my face doesn't leave with him this time, lingering for a while. It's still there as I finish my milkshake. Still there when I pay my bill and leave the warmth of the restaurant for the chilly Chicago day.

It's still there when I flop down on my bed to watch the evening news, and it's even wider when I see Vanya's face on the television, when the news anchor reports that he'd scored two goals in their game last night.

The guy I'm crushing on asks for my number, and I have a commercial shoot tomorrow. This might go down in history as the most interesting trip to Chicago I've ever had.

3

VANYA

I know I should play it cool, but ever since I ran into Katya last week in Chicago, I can't get her out of my mind. Though I felt an attraction to her the first time we met, I never would have acted on it. Our ages wouldn't have made anyone blink back home, but here, in America, I can't even imagine the things they'd say about us.

The night I met her, I was feeling homesick. Then, all of the sudden, there she is. A mature, beautiful, talented woman from Russia. Someone I could talk to without reservation, not only because we speak the same language, but also because she understands the fast-paced life of a professional athlete.

But seeing her randomly at a diner in Chicago feels like more than coincidence. It's as if our paths are supposed to cross.

I bring the gum wrapper to my nose and laugh as I inhale the minty scent, remembering how this was the only thing she had to write on. I lay back on my couch and dial the number on the paper.

"Hello?" she asks.

"Sunshine! How are you today?"

"Vanya! I'm well, thank you. It's nice to hear from you."

"Our meetings seem to get cut off too early. Now that I have your number I can bother you for as long as I want," I tease her.

"You don't bother me. I quite enjoy it."

"What's new in your world? What are you working on?"

"My forehand." She laughs, then continues. "Charlie says the two ways I can make my game better are my serve and my forehand. We've been working on both."

"You have a great coach."

"Oh!" she interjects. "I've also been working with a company to develop their next fragrance!"

I grab a glass out of the cabinet and fill it with tap water. "Really? That's fantastic!"

"As soon as my agent spoke to me about the opportunity, I had to run with it because—" She pauses. When she speaks again, some of the excitement is gone. "We both know how easy it is to get injured, Vanya. What if I lost my ability to play tennis tomorrow? What would I do?"

"I have faith that you would be amazing in anything you strive for."

It's an honest answer. She has a high level of drive, determination, and maturity. She'll be successful in anything with the right training.

"I agree," she says in a teasing voice. "Right now, I make more with endorsements than I do tennis. And while tennis is my number-one priority, I can't turn that money down."

"I understand," I say, nodding, though she can't see me over the phone.

When you grow up with nothing—no money, no way to move up in life, and no future change on the horizon—you grab every opportunity that arises and hold on tight.

"Do you enjoy that part? The modeling and endorsements?"

"I love it!" I can hear the genuine excitement in her tone. "But it has its downside. The media is all over me. I can't even get groceries without being photographed. I have no privacy."

"Maybe they think you're okay with the attention because you're on the cover of every magazine."

"Are you saying I brought it on myself?" There's a hint of annoyance in her voice, as if I'm accusing her. "Because I make the best of the attention, I deserve to have every part of my life photographed and analyzed?"

"That's not what I said, Katya. And it's not what I believe."

She sighs. "I know. I'm sorry. I just wish they would tone it down some, you know? Tennis is enough stress. Every match, every play, every serve is scrutinized. I don't like it, but I understand it. I don't understand the obsession with my personal life."

I do. She's absolutely gorgeous and she plays it up. Whether that's her doing or her management, I don't know. But the media has turned her into a sex symbol—a Lolita because of her age.

Should she standup and put a stop to it? I don't know that either.

We're not just athletes, we're products. And our product has an expiration date. If there's money being offered, better to take it while it's there.

"Yeah, I know. It's not as bad for me here in Detroit. It's a huge media market, but they really only care about how I perform. Like you, my every game, every shift, every play is scrutinized. I think Russians cared more about my personal life than people in here."

"I guess I was too young in Russia. No one really knew me yet."

"And now you're international news. Every girl wants to be you, and every man wants to be with you." As I walk into the living room, I'm mentally placing myself in that category. My pulse increases every time I think about how much I want to be with her.

She laughs. "It's a fantasy."

"Doesn't mean it's not true."

"Well, there's only one man I want to be with."

My heart races as I shuffle into the living room."Really?"

"Yes. Charlie. He's always got my back and he's the best coach I could ever ask for."

"Charlie, of course." I laugh, tension easing as I settle back into the cushions and rest my feet on the table, crossing them at the ankle.

"I'm going to be in Detroit next week. Maybe we can meet up for dinner. I mean, if you don't have plans or a game."

"Are you asking me out?" I ask with a smile, stretching one arm above my head.

"I'm not afraid to take charge, Vanya."

"Oh, I know!" This woman is not afraid of anything. "If you're going to be in town, I'll make time to see you while you're here. What day are you coming in?"

"I get in on Tuesday afternoon."

My brain pushes into overdrive as I try to remember our schedule for next week. Game on Monday and practice on Tuesday and Wednesday before we head out of town on Thursday. "Tuesday afternoon is perfect. I'll probably be home around five."

"I'm so excited," she gushes, bubbling with happiness. "It'll be perfect. Right before my meetings in New York."

"Wait. Are you're coming here just to see me?" I ask, confused.

"I'm a busy woman, Vanya. If I want to see you, I have to make time for it."

"So, you have no other obligations in Detroit than to be with me?" Excitement makes my voice raspy and thick.

She takes a deep breath, seemingly just as excited by the thought of it. "That's correct."

"Where are you staying?" I ask.

"I figured you could help me find a hotel when I got to Detroit. I don't know the area."

"Why don't you stay at my place." I want to spend every second with her, but I also know that's the excitement talking. I need to play it cool.

"Vanya," she says, finally showing a bit of restraint.

I get off the couch and walk back into the kitchen. "Katya, I don't mean it in any other way than giving you a place to stay. I have a four-bedroom house, and it's just me. You can stay in one of the guest rooms."

"A guest room, yes?" she teases.

"Take a cab to my house from the airport. I'd pick you up, but I'll be at the rink. I'll leave a key in the mailbox. We can grab dinner when I get home, and figure out where you will stay."

"Sounds good. I look forward to it."

"I'm excited to see you, Katya." I say before hanging up.

4

KATYA

As I sit in the cab on the ride to Vanya's house, butterflies rage in my stomach. I'm staying at his house. It seems so casual—a friend offering their home, but we both know it's more than that.

Out the window, I read every road sign waiting in anticipation as we approach the destination. My first impression of Detroit isn't a good one. It's dirty, desolate, and people drive way too fast on the highways. Then again, I suppose I would, too. I wouldn't want to be in this city very long. I hope Vanya lives in a suburb and not in the city.

Suddenly, the car turns onto a street named Iroquois, the road Vanya lives on. It's definitely still in the city, but it's a picturesque street lined with trees and gorgeous houses. I suppose that's a good compromise.

At quarter to five, the cab arrives in front of a huge, brick house with columns on each side of the porch. It has so much character and depth to it, unlike the cookie-cutter neighborhood in Florida where I live with my parents.

Vanya told me he'd be home around five. Which means I have about fifteen minutes to calm the swirling in my stomach. I run up the walkway, take the stairs two at a time, then reach into the mailbox for the key. As I fumble with the lock, I realize it's going to be harder than I thought. The butterflies only get crazier. As soon as I'm inside, I shut the door behind me, lean against it, and take a deep breath.

The house is obviously old, but the bright white walls stand out against the dark woodwork around the doors and windows. I've never seen such a charming place. It's beautifully decorated and so immaculate, I wonder if he has a maid come in or if he keeps it this way on his own. A silly part of me can't wait to figure it out. I want to learn all the little things about him.

I glance at the small, leather watch on my wrist, I'm so nervous—which is weird because being around Vanya calms me. Must be the anticipation of seeing him again.

Slowly, I walk around the living room, brushing the soft beige sofa with my fingertips. I sit gingerly on the couch, cross my legs, and put my hands in my lap. Then I uncross them and grab a magazine from the coffee table.

Vanya arrives home at exactly 5:03 p.m. I know because I've been sitting on the couch, absently flipping through a hockey magazine, and checking the clock above the television every five seconds. When he walks through the door, he looks even more handsome than I remember. It seems as if he's gotten a haircut recently, too.

"Katya!" he says, smiling as he enters.

I jump up and rush to him, throwing my arms around his neck. "Vanya!" Excitement hides the nervousness.

"You're gorgeous," he says as he scans my body from head to toe. He doesn't seem nervous at all. He's all confidence and compliments.

I tuck a piece of hair behind my ear and look up at him. "Thank you."

"I'm glad you found the place all right. Can I get you something to drink?" he asks, placing his keys on the table next to the door.

"No, thank you." My hand moves to my stomach, which rumbles with hunger instead of butterflies. "I'm actually starving. I haven't had a thing since breakfast."

"The guys keep raving about an amazing hot dog place not too far from here. Their specialties are chili dogs and fries. Wanna check it out?" he asks. There's so much enthusiasm in his voice, I couldn't say no even if I wanted to. And I certainly don't want to.

"I'm going to turn out like my *dedushka* if I keep hanging around you, Vanya," I say moving my hand forward as if I have a huge belly like my grandfather.

For two people who must maintain top physical condition, we seem to gravitate toward junk food when we're together. I'm not complaining. I love treating myself. I eat healthy ninety-five percent of the time. If five percent is junk, my workouts will take care of it.

"Don't pin that on me, Sunshine," he says, placing a hand on my back and guiding me out the door. "You were the one wolfing down a massive milkshake the last time I saw you."

I laugh and follow him to his car.

* * *

THE HOT DOG place is right next to another hot dog place. In fact, they share a wall. Vanya picks the one called Lafayette where you can see the food being prepared through the front windows. When he holds the door open, I go inside. It's a small place with a long counter and a few tables. And it's completely packed.

"Wow," I say, slightly surprised at the crowd. The food must be great because the décor is nonexistent. The walls are the weirdest thing. It looks like bathroom tile going up about three quarters up the wall. On top of that, they're lined with framed photos of people—many of them autographed. "This must be the place to be."

Amid the photos, there's a black sign with the scant offerings in white plastic letters. If you don't like hot dogs, fries, or chili, there's no reason to stay. Good thing I like all of them.

"What's a loose hamburger?" I ask Vanya, reading the menu out loud.

He shrugs.

"Well, then I have to try it," I say stepping forward to order. "Hi," I greet the man behind the counter, tucking my hair behind my ear.

"I'll have a Coney Island, a loose hamburger, and chili cheese fries, please."

After Vanya orders two Coneys and plain fries, the mustachioed man behind the counter looks at me as if he's trying to figure out if he knows me. "Are you—you're Ekaterina Novikova!"

I nod, flattered to be recognized. I can't stop the smile creeping onto my face. "How did you know?"

"We know our sports here." He points to the walls with his thumb. I notice the multiple posters of Detroit sports teams proudly displayed. Many of the photographs must be sports stars.

"That's Ivan Kravtsov with her!" one of the cooks behind him says.

"Kravtsov?" he addresses Vanya. "You've been in Detroit for years! How have you never been here before?"

"You are hidden gem," he tells them.

The man walks around the counter and throws one arm across my shoulders and the other across Vanya's. "Jimmy! Get the camera. We have two of the best athletes in the world right here. We need a picture for the wall!"

I can't stop smiling through the fuss. I have fans, and I'm used to being recognized on tour, but to be fussed over at a random hot dog place in Detroit is exciting. After we pose for a few photos, Jimmy clears two places at the counter for Vanya and I.

"I didn't expect that kind of welcome," Vanya says. "Makes me glad I waited to eat here."

Despite just getting settled, Jimmy places our plates in front of us. It's the fastest service I've ever had in my life.

"You don't like the attention?" I ask, popping a chili and cheese covered fry into my mouth. It's absolutely delicious. So much so, that I make an audible, "Mmmmm" sound.

Vanya's right eyebrow raises. "That good?"

I can only nod in answer because I've just shoved three more fries into my mouth. It's not very lady-like, but they're so good, I can't help it.

"I'm glad I waited because I'm happy you were with me for it." He glances at the walls. "There are thousands of photos with me and my teammates all over the place. But this will be the only photo with you and I."

"For now," I tell him. "But we'll have plenty of time for photos, Vanya."

"Yes?" he asks.

"Of course!" I smile and slap his leg lightly. My grin falters as I realize Vanya might not think the same way. "Unless, you don't want to continue seeing me."

"Are you kidding me?" Vanya reels back as if offended. "I love every minute with you. You ground me."

His response warms my heart. I wipe my mouth off on a napkin before I speak. "Ground you?"

He leans back. "It's been difficult here since I arrived. It's hard not knowing anyone and not being able to communicate as effectively as I'd like. I have hockey in common with my teammates, but our backgrounds are so different. They don't know what life was like where we're from."

"Have you had anyone to talk to, Vanya?" I grab his hand and hold it with both of mine.

"I actually became really good friends with my translator. The one the team hired for me when I arrived." He laughs and shakes his head. "He's a good guy. A professor at a local university. He was born in Russia but came here as a child. Still, he's someone I can speak to freely."

"It feels good to have someone to talk to, doesn't it?"

He nods. "That's why I like being around you. Growing up as athletes in a severe system, we have similar backgrounds. You know what it feels like to have intense pressure on your shoulders. And we can speak without miscommunication."

"Well, language-wise, yes," I tease, picking up my fork, ready to dig into the main course. "But women and men can be on different wavelengths."

He places his hand on my back. "What about us? Are we on different wavelengths?"

"After this conversation, I don't think so." I point to his plate with my fork. "Now eat before it gets too cold. I have a feeling cold Coney dogs aren't as magical."

Vanya nods. "You're eating a hot dog with a fork?"

"Look at it!" I say, glancing down at my plate. The bun is filled with so much chili I can't even see the actual hot dog. And there's a line of mustard and onions to top it off. "I can't possibly pick it up without everything dripping all over me."

Vanya glances at my chest, rather than the food. "I'd be happy to help you clean up."

"I bet you would," I say before clearing my throat and getting to work on my meal. He smiles at my eagerness.

"Cheers," he says, raising his overflowing fork. I tap it with my own, and we both take our first bites.

"Oh my God, this is fantastic!" I exclaim. "It's the best thing I've tasted in forever." I wanted to catch Vanya's reaction, but instead, I dig in for another bite.

"Better than milkshakes?" he asks.

"Mmmm." I shrug, then hold up a finger until I finish chewing. "It's a totally different taste. Like comparing apples to oranges."

"Does your coach know you wolf down the milkshakes and Coney dogs at every chance?" he asks quietly, looking around as if Charlie will pop out from a corner.

"This stays between us," I say, lowering my voice and throwing a glance over my shoulder. "I tell him I eat salad at every meal."

"I bet he's not fooled." He laughs again.

I join him this time. Other people in the diner steal glances at us, probably wondering what the people speaking a foreign language are laughing about.

"Do they even serve salad here?" Vanya asks, craning his neck to see the menu.

"They don't. Just junk food," I reply. "Tell me something, Vanya. What's your guilty pleasure?"

The question makes him choke. His eyes bulge, and he brings a napkin to his mouth.

"Food, Vanya! Food," I confirm, rolling my eyes and folding my arms across my chest. "You're like a fourteen-year-old boy."

He bursts out laughing. I like the way he laughs—deep, throaty, and it makes his eyes crinkle at the corners.

"My guilty pleasure, Ekaterina, is ice cream." He lowers his voice and brings his mouth to my ear. "In a cone. I enjoy sweeping my tongue across it and letting it slide down my throat."

"Ice cream, yes?" I swallow hard, shifting in my seat and squeezing my muscles to hold back the lust pulsing between my legs.

"There's an ice cream place around the corner. We should stop there before we head back to my place."

"I'd like that," I tell him, trying to keep my composure. I want nothing more than to be with Vanya tonight. I want to shove him onto the couch, crawl on top of him, and make out for hours. But I want to take things slow. I'm already head over heels for him. I don't want to go too fast and get my heart broken. "But I'm staying in a hotel tonight."

He doesn't miss a beat. "Whatever makes you comfortable, Sunshine. No pressure here."

Once we finish, we set our napkins on our plates, and Vanya throws cash on the counter. "Come on, let's go check out those ice cream flavors."

5

VANYA

Saying goodbye to Katya last night gave me massive blue balls, but I'd never rush her into doing anything she wasn't ready for. When I woke up with massive morning wood, I had to relieve it before my morning run. Running around the neighborhood with my shorts tented might get me arrested; though in Detroit, I'm not sure.

After my run, I'm tired, sweaty, and in dire need of a shower. Probably has just as much to do with the run as it does my thoughts about Katya. I couldn't stop thinking about her. We had a great night eating and talking. The best night I've had in a while, actually.

I head straight for the master bathroom, removing my soaked shirt and tossing it on the tile floor. That's when I hear the doorbell. I'm not expecting anyone, so I ignore it. But it goes off again as I'm turning the water on.

"Damn it!" I let out a loud sigh and shut the faucet off before heading to the stairs. When my impatient visitor presses the bell again, I yell, "I'm coming!"

With furrowed brows and a deep frown, I yank open the door hoping my face scares off the unexpected caller. When I see Katya standing there, holding paper bags from the market down the road, my frown quickly dissolves. She's looking as beautiful as ever in a flannel shirt tucked into designer jeans.

"Why are you naked?" she asks, confused.

"I'm not," I begin, then glance down at my shirtless chest and chuckle. "I was just about to hop in the shower."

"Are you going to keep standing there, showing off your sexy physique to the neighbors, or are you going to invite me in?" she asks, holding the bags up.

Now, I'm the one confused. She was supposed to be on a plane to New York this morning. "Please, come on in." I move back giving her room to enter. "I'm just surprised. What are you doing here?"

"I wasn't ready to leave you yet." She pauses to kiss me quickly, almost as if she's not sure she should. Then she strolls toward the kitchen, dropping the paper bags on the table in the dining room. "Is it a good surprise?"

"Absolutely." I follow her to the kitchen where she's unpacking the bags. She pulls out meat, onions, and noodles.

"What's cooking?" I ask, placing my hands on her hips and peering over her shoulder.

"No offense, Vanya, but you stink." She waves me back. "Go upstairs and shower. By the time you get back down, I'll be almost finished making dinner."

"Okay, okay!" I hold my hands up and back away, watching her dance around as she unloads groceries. "I look forward to it."

"Need someone to wash your back?" She calls over her shoulder.

I pause in the doorway. "You're more than welcome to join me, Sunshine."

She shakes a bag of noodles like it's a maraca. "I might surprise you."

* * *

IT TAKES me less than fifteen minutes to shower and dress. I don't want to miss out on too much time with her since I don't know how long she has here.

As I race down the stairs, I almost pass her up, thinking she'd still be in the kitchen. Instead, she's standing in front of a painting in my hallway—one of many throughout the house.

"You're into art?" She turns to me.

"No, not exactly. That came with the house," I reply, thrusting my hands into the pockets of my shorts and leaning against the wall. I smile as I watched her admire the oversized painting.

"What does it mean?" she asks with eyes full of curiosity.

"I bought this house—and everything in it—from the owner of the Chargers. He has," I lift my eyes to the ceiling as I count. "I don't know how many properties he has. I think he owns most of Detroit."

"So, this art means nothing to you?" She tilts her head.

"Well, I mean, I did research this one. The name of that painting is 'War.'" I clear my throat and move closer to her. "It's about two lovers, warriors, who fought against the society they lived in because of the love they had for each other, to protect that love and be free," I add as I trace the delicate brush strokes on the piece of art.

Her gorgeous eyes meet mine, and my heart speeds up. "Did they win the war? The war of love?"

"I think that's up to interpretation," I say, brushing her hair behind her shoulder so I can see her face. "What do you think? Do you think they won?"

"I don't know for certain, but what I do know is that love is freedom. People should be allowed to love freely," she replies, looking from me to the painting. She swallows thickly, as if nervous—or excited.

"I agree. What if obligations get in the way?" I cup her cheek in my palm.

She closes her eyes for a brief moment, seemingly enjoying the feel of my hand. When she opens them, she says, "Nothing gets in the way of real love. You make time to see people. If you really love someone, you make them a priority."

I lean closer, so close I'm breathing her breath when I whisper. "Am I a priority?"

She nods, her lips brushing mine when she says, "Am *I* priority?"

Instead of answer, I close the miniscule distance between us, and press my lips to hers. She wraps her arms around my neck and pulls me into her warm, lithe body. My fingers graze her hips, as I gently hold her in place and increase the pressure on her mouth. I part her lips with my tongue and explore gently. She responds with a soft moan and moves her fingers to my hair, tugging on the roots as she sinks into my arms.

When she pulls away her plump, pink lips glisten. Between the taste of her and the delicious aroma in the air, my stomach growls with want.

"Is dinner ready?" I ask, looking over her head toward the kitchen.

She slaps my shoulder. "After that amazing kiss, all you care about is food?"

"Don't worry, Katya." I pull her hips toward me, knowing she can feel how hungry I am for her by the erection pressing against her belly. "Even after we eat, I'll still be starving for you."

"It's ready," she says, grabbing my hand and pulling me to the kitchen.

While Katya dishes out dinner, I remove two wine glasses from the cabinet. "How did the Glonex commercial go?" I ask.

She sets each plate on the table and sits down. "It was wonderful," she gushes, smiling brightly. "I absolutely love modeling, Vanya. It makes me feel beautiful and free."

"Free?" I ask, scanning the wine cooler for a specific kind. Once I find it, I grab the bottle opener and glasses and bring them to the table.

"With tennis, everything is structured, you know. I have to remain calm and perfectly poised all the time. The only ways I can be myself are in the outfits I wear. And even those have to be a certain brand."

"A certain brand that pays you a lot of money to have you endorsing them." I set the glasses down on the table.

"Of course, they do, Vanya. Have you seen how good I look in tennis skirts?" She stands up, places both hands on her hips, and shakes them playfully.

"Supermodels have nothing on you," I reply as both of us laugh. She sits back down.

I hold the opener over the neck of the wine bottle, push down on the lever, then pull it up. The cork comes out with ease. "You're the face of a major sports brand, not too many Russians can say that."

"They say it's because of my looks, not my play." She pushes noodles around on her plate.

"You won a Grand Slam two years in a row. You're the second ranked female tennis player in the world. Whoever 'they' are can shove it up their ass."

There are always going to be people who want to downplay her talent because she's beautiful, but her success on the court isn't something that can be faked. You don't win on looks.

She snorts then wipes her mouth with her napkin. "What do you have there?"

"You like wine, yes?"

"Yes, I like wine."

I pour her a glass before filling mine. "This was a gift from Mr. Popovic, the Chargers owner, when I arrived in America. I always thought it was sad to drink such a great wine alone, so I saved it for a special occasion."

"That's so sweet, Vanya," she says genuinely.

"Let's make a toast," I clear my throat as I slide into the seat beside her. "Let's make a toast to you, a beautiful, talented woman, fulfilling her dreams." We clink our glasses and sip.

"We should toast to you, too."

"Toast to me? Why?" I ask.

"You made it out of the USSR. You have this huge house. You play for a great team. You have everything we never had growing up. You're living the American dream."

She's right. I have everything—or do I? Why is there a gnawing reminder that the American dream isn't my dream?

"What is it?" Katya asks. She's quick to notice the change in countenance.

"Nothing," I reply, quickly pushing the thoughts aside as I raise the glass to my lips again. I don't want to ruin the moment. "The wine's really good, yes?"

"Best wine I've ever had."

"You want more?" I point to her glass, which is nearly empty.

"Please." She happily slides it toward me. "So, tell me something, Vanya." She looks at me through thick lashes, coated in mascara. "Do you have many women in your life?"

She brings the glass to her lips and crosses her legs at the knee as she waits for my answer. Her sultry gaze sends chills up and down my spine.

I've dated a few girls since arriving in Detroit, but nothing serious. Mostly just someone to spend time with during the off season. I don't even try to mess with a relationship while I'm playing. There's no time to give a woman the attention she deserves.

The connection with Katya was instant, from the very first moment I laid eyes on her. She's irresistibly beautiful, confident, and extremely fun to be around. She is just so vibrant and full of life.

"Are you counting in your head?" Her voice jolts me out of my thoughts, her sexy blue eyes meeting mine again. "Is it that many?"

"It's not many at all, Katya," I finally reply. "I have no one in my life at the moment."

"No?" She reaches out and tickles my ribs. "Not one woman?"

I catch her hands, pull her into my lap and wrap my arms around her. Then I nuzzle my nose into her neck. "There is this one woman."

She laughs and tilts her neck, giving me access to cover it with kisses.

It's getting hot and heavy, when Katya puts her hands on my chest. "I have to go," she says breathlessly.

"You want to leave?" I ask. "Now?"

"It's not that I *want* to leave." She clutches my T-shirt and pulls me closer. "But if I don't, I won't be able to control myself."

"I am one hundred percent okay with that."

She laughs. "I need more time."

"I'll wait as long as you need," I tell her, placing a kiss on her forehead. "Come on, I'll drive you to your hotel."

6

VANYA

My eyes jolt open, awakened by the phone. There's no trace of light, not even the dull early morning glow that usually seeps through hotel-room curtains. With half-open eyes, I turn over and check the small clock on the nightstand. Ugh! 4:56 a.m.

It has to be a wrong number. We rarely get calls to our hotel room when we're on road trips. Mainly because no one even know where we stay.

Though there's an odd feeling in my stomach, I'm not going to dwell on it. Maybe my roommate, Petr Novotný will answer. With that prospect in my head, I reposition the duvet and try to go back to sleep. I've barely shut my eyes when the phone rings again.

"Who the hell is calling at four in the morning?" I mutter to myself, pulling the duvet over my head this time, trying to ignore it.

The sound of the second ring still echoes in my ear when it goes off a third time. I have every intention of ignoring the call, hoping the person at the other end realizes they've dialed the wrong number. But when it keeps ringing, my brain goes into panic mode.

A call at five a.m. is either the wrong number or something urgent.

"Damn it," I sigh as I shove the duvet off my body, the cold air hitting my bare chest as I sit up and reach over to grab the receiver.

"This better be good," I say as I answer, throwing an annoyed glance at Novotný who's dead to the world.

"We have a problem, Vanya, a big problem." The words are urgent, and even though the person doesn't introduce himself, I know the firm voice of my agent—and long-time friend—Kirya.

"Problem?" I ask. My mind races, thinking of anything that could have gone wrong over the past few days or weeks. I couldn't pinpoint any, unless it had to do with my sister. "Is Stasya okay?"

"Yes, she's fine."

I wipe my forehead and relax a bit.

"This is about you and Katya," he continues. "In a few hours, your relationship is going to be all over the newspapers."

"You called me at five a.m. to tell me my relationship is going to be in the newspapers." I yawn loudly in his ear. "It couldn't have waited until eight?"

"She was photographed leaving your place last week," he says, throwing random information at me like pieces of a puzzle, and I'm having a hard time putting them together. I'm really confused at why he's so concerned. "Are you listening to me, Vanya?"

"Yes, I'm listening," I reply, clearing my throat and wiping my sleepy eyes. "You'll have to explain what's going on because I'm confused," I confess. He's moving too fast for me this early.

"We have a scandal on our hands."

"What's the scandal, Kirya?" I swallow hard as I speak, my fingers reaffirming the grip on the receiver.

"A seventeen-year-old was photographed leaving your private residence. You were also spotted together in Chicago. The media is going to rail you. She's underage, Vanya." He's taken the time to explain, yet his concern is still clear as mud.

"What does it matter? She turns eighteen next month. And—" I rub my forehead again. "What does it matter?"

"It matters because the media here is always trying to create drama. They aren't going to say 'Oh, they're Russian and that's normal for that culture.' They're going to say, 'He's a pedophile,'" he replies.

Using that word feels like he threw cold water on my face.

He's right. It's something I didn't think of because I don't think of Kayta as a child. She's a woman—a professional. She's been away from her parents—on her own in the tennis circuit—for years. We're close because we have so much in common. I'm not a monster who preys on children.

Back home, a twenty-five-year old man being in a relationship with a seventeen-year-old wasn't a big deal; in fact, it's very normal. It's not about age, it's about stability. Russian women don't want men with future potential, they want men who are established.

In America, though, they have a different culture and a way of doing things, and even though Katya and I are not American, it's not going to matter much to the media. Kirya is right, we have a really big problem.

"What do we do now?"

"You're going to have to lay low until she turns eighteen."

"It's so stupid! You don't just turn into an adult because your age changes."

"We both know that, but it's a magic number here. A *legal* number," he emphasizes. "You must promise me you won't see her again until she turns eighteen."

"I promise." I pause, then continue quickly. "I'm not attracted to children, Kirya."

"For fuck's sake, Vanya. I know that! Zhenya went through the same thing, and she was sixteen when they dated. We both know he's not interested in children either. He's interested in hot, Russian models, like any warm-blooded male."

After Kirya's call, I can't sleep, so I get up quietly and get ready to go to the arena early. I plan on pounding the treadmill and weights until morning skate.

* * *

"Dude, I'm sorry about the news," Simmons, says when we take the ice. "They make everything sound so seedy."

I skate to his left side, reaching for a rogue puck near the boards. "If you listen to the press, it's like they think I'm prowling high schools for dates."

"Right?" Novotný chimes in from behind me. He places his helmet on his head. "Athletes at our level have been adults since we were teenagers. We're old enough to get drafted and sign contracts, but not old enough to date each other. It's fucked."

"Don't let it get to you, V," Simmons bumps my shoulder with his glove. "It'll blow over as soon as she turns eighteen. Then you'll turn into their power couple."

Suddenly, I realize I may have more in common with my teammates than I originally gave them credit for. We may have grown up in different environments, but we're all professionals. We all had to conduct ourselves as adults before we turned any technical age.

I squirt water into my mouth, drop the bottle back in the holder as I spit, and hit the ice, ready to put this drama behind me and get my head ready for tonight's game against the New York Americans.

* * *

After the game, I head back to the hotel instead of grab a drink with the boys. They tried to lure me by saying they'll go to the Russian Dining Room, but not even that can sway me. I want to talk to Katya to see how she's feeling about everything.

Kirya was right, we're all over the news. He told me to ignore all the drama and go about my regular schedule as if nothing were happening, so I did. But I have a gnawing feeling Katya wasn't able to. She does a great job of ignoring the stories, but I know it gets to her.

When I get to my room, there's a message from her saying she wants to talk and she'll be here at eleven. I'm relieved she's coming. We're in this together.

"She should be here by now," I mumble to myself as I check the time.

It's 11:13 p.m. I keep pacing, biting my nails, my heart racing as I wait for her to arrive. I should have gone to her hotel. But there are more paparazzi outside her place than at the one the guys and I stay at.

"Finally!" I jump up as soon as I hear the knock. "Come on in," I say hurriedly, as she steps in. You never know who may have followed her, lurking behind with their camera ready. "Are you okay?" I ask.

She looks exhausted. Her usual, bubbly smile is missing, and her eyes are rimmed with red.

"I don't know, Vanya," she says, running her fingers through her lifeless locks as she drops onto the couch. She buries her face in her hands. "I've gotten dozens of calls today. It's all so overwhelming." She sighs deeply, sounding tired and defeated. "Did you read the papers this morning?"

"No. I'm trying to avoid them," I reply, sitting next to her.

"Well, I've seen them. Charlie brought some to me. It's a scandal, Vanya. A man with an underage girl. They can't let that part go. I'll be eighteen in two months, but they make you sound like—" She lowers her head and inspects her nails. "It's ridiculous that they make such a big deal over nothing," she adds, huffing and rubbing her eyes.

I place a hand over hers. "Is it nothing?"

She slowly turns her head toward me, silence hanging in the air as we stare at each other.

"What do you mean?" she asks. The leather squeaks when she adjusts her position to turn to me.

"Look Katya, I know we have a lot of things to talk about, and I know things seems really crazy right now. But ever since the moment we ran into each other in Chicago, I've had only one thing on my mind." I hold her gaze as I speak. I want her to know everything is true, and it comes from my heart.

"What is it, Vanya?" she asks gently, the words coming out in a whisper.

I shift closer to her on the couch, closing the gap between us as I take her hand in mine. "You, Katya. All I can think about is you. Day and night. During games. While I'm—while I'm doing anything."

She stares at me, blinking a few times as if trying to understand, but not speaking.

The silence is killing me. I want her to say something, anything—even if it's rejection. I can handle rejection. I can't handle not knowing how she feels.

All of a sudden, her hands are on my face, cupping it gently. She leans closer, so close I can feel her warm breath on my face. Then she kisses me. It's a quick touching of lips at first, very brief before she pulls back, her eyes searching mine as if seeking my approval.

"Can I?" she whispers.

"Always," I say before she kisses me again. It's longer this time, more passionate. She presses her lips to mine, our mouths moving together as she pulls me even closer. Her lips are soft, delicate, and taste like bubblegum. My mouth has never touched anything better. Her tongue flicks at my lips, seeking entrance.

"Mmm," she moans softly as I open for her, our tongues clashing as the passion begins to consume us. I kiss her back, matching her energy. She tugs my hair as she clutches it. Things are progressing faster now, mouths and hands exploring each other.

"Wait, we should stop," she says, breaking away from the kiss, ending the moment just as quickly as it started.

"What's wrong?" I ask.

"We can't do this, Vanya. I thought I could, but—" She touches her lips with her fingertips. She breaks eye contact and backs away. "I'm sorry."

"What's wrong? You don't feel the same way?" I ask. I thought we were on the same page. All of our interactions—every smile, every touch—has led us to this moment.

"No, Vanya, I feel the same way. I promise, I do. But we can't do this right now. We can't be together." She faces me, making eye contact again as she says the words.

"Why?" I swallow hard.

"We're all over the papers already, and we've haven't even started dating officially." She throws her hands in the air. "It's just—a lot of things are holding us back."

"What? What things are holding us back?"

"I just don't see a way this could work." Her voice shakes, and tears well up in her eyes.

"We can make this work. It's going to take a lot of effort and some sacrifice from both of us, but we can do it." There's confidence in my words. I don't see this as a situation that needs to tear us apart.

"There are a lot of things at stake here. My career, your career. Charlie said I could lose my endorsements," she replies.

"Don't worry about the media. We're going to have to ignore them for the rest of our lives. They make news from nothing to create an uproar because it sells papers." I grab her hands, imploring her to understand. "I don't care about any of the bullshit they're reporting. All I care about is you, Katya."

She lifts her eyes to the ceiling, sniffing as her eyelashes flutter, trying to blink back tears. "I know you care about me, and I care about you, too. But this can't work, Vanya." As she says my name, the first tear breaks free, trickling down her face. "I'm sorry, I have to go."

She rises quickly and leaves without looking back.

"Katya!" I call after her. The world seems to stop for a few seconds. The back of my throat feels dry and irritated. The words sting, hurting in ways I could have never imagined.

At first, I think about running after her, trying to convince her that we could make it work, but I don't. She's freaked out, upset, and thinks this is bigger than it is. Nothing I say right now will change her mind. I just sit there, stuck to the couch, thinking of her words and thinking of how I lost her over media pressure—something so stupid and seemingly insignificant.

Something so stupid that will be a part of our lives for as long as either of us is in the spotlight.

7

KATYA

While in Vanya's room, my chest tightened and it felt like the walls were closing in. As soon as I'm outside, I breathe in the cool air and rush to the curb, raising my arm to hail a cab.

"Four hundredth block of Madison Avenue, please," I reply as I hurriedly get into the car.

"You know the number?" he asks.

"Umm, no. It's a hotel, the Castle." It's getting harder to breathe, and when I look out the window, I can barely see with the tears clouding my eyes.

"I got ya," he confirms in a thick New York accent. "You okay, ma'am?"

"Yes, j-just drive, please." My voice shakes so badly, the words are barely audible.

I had been holding it in since I told Vanya he and I couldn't be together, holding back the tears from streaming down my face as I flagged down a cab. But now that I'm heading back to the solace of my own hotel room, and the driver's attention is solely on the road ahead, I can finally let myself go. I lean back into the seat, rest my head on the window, and allow the tears to stream down my face.

I sob quietly as thoughts of Vanya, the only man I've ever fallen hard for, swim around in my head. I don't know where I summoned the courage to break his heart, to break my own heart, but I had to.

I can't have him thrown off his game over some stupid stories in the press. I can't have him thinking about me instead of thinking about his career.

I blamed it all on the press, the American press, who love to ruin whoever they consider celebrities. They killed off the flame before it even got a chance to ignite. The papers and media portray Vanya as a predator and me as a helpless girl who needed saving. They said because I'm still seventeen—underage in American laws—they make it appear like Vanya is a monster.

"You said the Castle, right?" the driver, who had been quiet since we started moving, asks.

His question draws me out of my thoughts. "Yes," I reply, blinking fast, wiping my cheeks with the back of my hands.

"We're here," he replies, stopping in front of the massive brick building. The full name of the luxury hotel is, The Castle New York, which makes total sense because I feel like a princess when I stay here.

"Thanks," I reply, wiping my eyes one last time before stepping out of the car.

"It's a beautiful hotel," he says as his eyes admire the place.

"Here you go." I hand him some bills, without waiting to find out how much the fare was.

After entering the hotel, I race up the grand staircase, not because I need to take them to get to my room—there are elevators on the main floor—but because I can't be here without taking them. I don't see how anyone could stay at a place called a 'Castle' that has something they call a 'grand staircase,' without using it.

When I walk into the sitting area between my room and Charlie's, he's there, sitting on the couch, with a bottle of flavored-water beside him. "You're back," he says, looking up with a smile. His expression quickly turns to concern. "Are you okay?"

Charlie is more like a second father than a coach. We've spent more time together over the last few years than I have with my own parents. He knew me before I became a star, before all the fame, glitz, and glamour.

"Yeah, why?" I reply, sniffing as I try to force a smile. I side step him and go straight to my door. "I'll be right back, Charlie. I need to use the restroom."

The last thing I want is questions about why I've been crying. When he agreed to let me come to New York to shoot a commercial for an international make up brand, I told him I'd be completely focused on preparing for my match this weekend. He'd know immediately if—

"You went to see him, didn't you?" he asks, interrupting my thoughts.

"What are you talking about?" I gather myself quickly but don't turn to face him.

"Don't play that game with me, Katya. I know you too well," he says gently, almost as if he's pleading with me, begging me to tell him what was going on. "I see your eyes, I know you've been crying." He gets up and walks towards me. "Did you go to see Vanya?"

"Yes, I went to see him," I say quietly. Then I take a deep breath and will myself not to start crying again, but I can feel the tears well up.

"Are you okay?"

I pause before speaking, thinking of what to say. If I tell him I'm okay, yet lock myself away in my room, he'll know I'm not. Hell, even if I try to keep it together, Charlie will know. He'll know in my demeanor. He'll know during training. I might as well just bypass the drama and come clean.

"I'm not okay, Charlie," I turn around, letting the tears stream down my face. This time, I let myself go, sobbing louder than I had in the cab.

"Come here," Charlie pulls me into an embrace, stroking my back as I let it all out. He consoles me for a few minutes, saying nothing, just allowing me to cry. "Do you want to talk about it?"

"Yes," I reply, sniffing as I break away from the embrace.

When I start wiping at my tears my fingers, Charlie leads me to the couch. He grabs a box of tissue off the table and hands it to me sitting down. "What happened?"

"He's in town for a game. So, I went to his hotel. I know it wasn't a good idea to go see him, but I had to, I needed to see him." I sniff as I speak, still trying to blink back the tears as the words roll off my lips.

"I understand, Katya. When you said you were going out, I didn't try to stop you or go with you. I knew you were going to see him," he says. "Was Vanya upset about everything that's going on?"

"Yes. He was angry and annoyed with the media. It's ridiculous that we can't just live our lives. Don't we have enough pressure?"

Charlie nods.

"He—Vanya told me he has feelings for me," I tell him as if he doesn't already know.

"And you have feelings for him, too, don't you?" he asks.

"I wouldn't be crying like this if I didn't have feelings for him, Charlie. I haven't been able to keep him out of my head since the first day I saw him at that party you invited me to in Detroit." I wipe my face again. "Do you remember that party?" I ask wistfully, smiling as the memories from the night we met flood my head. Everything still seems so fresh: the way he spoke to me, the way he smiled, the things we talked about.

"I told him we couldn't be together though." I lean back into the couch, a failed attempt to send back the coming tears.

"Why did you tell him that?" he asks calmly. He's treating me like a fragile doll, and I'm not. Just because I'm letting my emotions out doesn't mean I'm going to have a total breakdown.

"You brought the papers to me this morning, Charlie. You intercepted the calls from the media. You saw the horrible things they said. We haven't even started dating yet. It's a distraction," I say, wiping the tears forming at the corner of my eyes away.

"Are you sure that's the reason?" Charlie leans back into the couch and folds his arms across his chest.

"What do you mean?" I ask.

"Are you sure that the reason you told him you couldn't be

together is because of the press? And because of the fact that it could affect your careers?" he asks, shrugging his shoulders. I'm beginning to get where he was driving at.

"Yes, I guess."

"Come on Katya, we both know that's not the reason," Charlie says, bumping my shoulder with his, as if trying to get me to confess.

He's right though, that wasn't the reason we couldn't be together. I'd lied to myself, lied to him, tried to convince myself that the reason Vanya and I couldn't be together was because of the media and the fact that our careers were at stake.

"You're right, Charlie. It's because I'm scared," I say, finally telling him the truth as I wipe tears from the corner of my eyes again.

"What's there to be scared about?"

"Everything!" I jump up. "When we were all over the news this morning, it annoyed me. Most of the time I can brush it off, but this really got to me because of how horrible they were to him. And how they make us out to be terrible people because we like each other. Does he deserve that, Charlie? Does he deserve to be raked through the mud just for spending time with me?"

"No."

I rake my fingers through my hair and pace the room. "It all happened so quickly. I met him once and I couldn't get him out of my head. I told myself all this time that it was nothing but a crush—a stupid teenage crush. But when I got to his place and he told me how he felt about me, I realized that I'd been denying it. And now it's real." I stop pacing and look at Charlie. "And I freaked out because I can't handle what's to come."

"And what's to come?" he asks.

"The storm, Charlie. Being with him is going to take a lot of effort and sacrifice, and I'm not sure I'm up to that," I tell him. As soon as the words leave my lips, I feel bad, as if I shouldn't be so selfish.

"There's always going to be a storm, my dear. That's how your life will be as long as you're in the public eye."

"I know Charlie, but I don't want to get hurt. I don't want to hurt him, either," I tell him.

Fear. That's the real reason. Fear of getting hurt. Fear of hurting him. Fear of what else the media will say about him and how it will affect his mind and career. We lead busy lives. We don't live in the same city. We're dedicated to different things—it will all get in the way.

"He's a big boy. He can handle himself." When I huff, Charlie leans forward and gives me a gentle smile. "You're never going to know if you don't give it a shot. And I know you want to give it a shot."

"Have you been listening to anything I've said?" I ask throwing my hands in the air. Sometimes I feel like he doesn't listen to me.

Charlie gets up and crosses the room to stand in front of me. He places his hands on my shoulders. "Look, Katya, I don't know what you want me to say, but I'll tell you this. You're hurt already. Hurt because you really like him and you broke things off before you even got the chance to see how amazing it could be. Don't make this into something you'll regret down the road. Why not just give it a shot and see where it leads?" He leans forward and places a kiss on my forehead before shuffling to his room.

I'm lucky to have a coach like Charlie. He knows me inside and out—sometimes more than I know myself. When he gives me advice I listen, yet, if either of my parents said the same thing, I wouldn't listen.

"Damn it," I mumble.

What in the world did I do?

8

KATYA

"In three... two....one, shoot!"

The music comes on, the fans start blowing, flashing lights, and the cameras start clicking. Today, I'm shooting a spread for a new tennis apparel line.

"Turn to the left. Good!" the photographer yells as I run through the poses we practiced earlier. I'm all glammed up for the shoot, yet still in my signature high pony tail. I'm sporting exclusives from a yet-to-be released collection, wielding a gold-colored tennis racket.

"I'm not feeling this," Monica, the director of the shoot, yells as the cameras keep clicking, the lights flashing.

I'm doing the best I can; smiling the way they taught me to smile, posing the way they taught me to pose. But even I know I'm off, I can feel it in my forced smile and dull eyes. I'm not enjoying the shoot as I normally do.

"Alright, alright, stop the music, cut the fans." Monica waves her hands. The entire place goes silent. "What's wrong, Katya? Your energy has been off since we started shooting," She speaks quickly, pushing her glasses up her nose with almost every word she said.

"I'm sorry, I ju—"

Monica places her hands on my shoulders. "Is it that time of the month?"

"What? No!" I shake my head and wiggle out of her arms. Placing my hands on my hips, I try to gain composure. "I have a million things on my mind for the match coming up. Can I get a quick break? Two minutes, please?"

"You need a break? Let's take a break," she says, then turns around to address the crew. "Five-minute break everyone!" she yells out to them before turning back to me. "You get five minutes, Katya, because I love that accent." She winks before gingerly stepping off the stage, her exceptionally high heels making 'click,' 'click' sounds as she walks away.

I roll my eyes and jump off the set; Charlie's waiting for me by the time I walk away from the lights.

"Are you okay?" he asks as he hands me a bottle of water.

"Yeah, sure," I reply, tucking the racket under my arm.

He raises an eyebrow. There's a mix of concern and curiosity in his eyes. "Are you sure?"

"Yes," I shrug and bring the bottle to my lips. "Why are you asking?"

"Well, Monica just said your energy is off." He folds his arms and leans against the wall. He still has that look in his eyes.

"And?"

"Your energy has been off ever since you broke things off with Vanya." He shrugs. "Seems interesting."

"You think what Monica said about the shoot has to do with Vanya?" I ask as I twist the cap to close the bottle.

"That's exactly what I think," he replies. "You were also off during most of our training sessions, so something's definitely up with you."

He's right, of course. My mind hasn't been right since that night in New York. I haven't been able to get Vanya out of my head since that day.

I had tried, tried to distract myself, but the harder I tried to get him out of my head, the more I thought of him.

"For a coach who wants me to be focused on training, you sure care a lot about something that could be a huge distraction."

"Seems to me, it's already a distraction. And I much prefer happily distracted Katya. Happy Katya is fierce, strong, and gets her shit done because she knows she can do whatever she wants in her free time."

I laugh. "That's me all the time, Charlie. I've never let you down."

"And I've never let you down." He pushes himself off the wall and glances at the direction of the clicking of Monica's heels returning to the set. "The Chargers are in town. They're playing the Panthers tonight. I'm pretty sure I can get Katya Novikova into the game."

"Times up people! We start shooting again in thirty seconds," Monica calls.

"Go get 'em, Tiger!" Charlie takes the water bottle from me and pushes me toward the set.

It's exactly what I have to do—both on the set and tonight.

* * *

I ADJUST my wool hat and rub my hands together before shoving them back into the pockets of my cardigan, wishing I would have brought a pair of gloves. When I left my house, I underestimated how cold it was outside. The wind whips at my face as I rush to the arena. I check my watch. A few minutes past nine p.m. Vanya's game will be over soon, unless it goes into overtime.

All day, I'd thought about what Charlie said, and at the last minute, I decided to take his advice. I bought a ticket to the game, hoping I could use my celebrity status to get a pass to wait outside the visiting team's locker room. Have I figured out what I'm going to say once I see him? No, but everything I'm going to tell him will be the truth.

I wait in the hallway near the locker room door for about fifteen minutes before the press starts filing out. I turn to the wall and shake my hair in front of my face so I'm not recognized. When the coast is clear, I turn around and stare at the door. As minutes tick by, it feels like watching a pot of boiling water.

It's twenty more minutes before any players come out. A few of them walk out together, laughing and chatting happily, but most guys slip out alone with their collars up and rush down the hallway without looking around. Vanya comes out with two other players.

"Vanya!" I call out, waving at him. "Vanya!" I call again, louder this time as I finally get his attention. He says something to his teammates that I can't hear, but he heads in my direction.

"What are you doing here?" he asks, giving me a forced smile. I hate seeing it, but I understand it. I was emotional and volatile, and I didn't listen to him or trust him, pretty much everything a Russian man hates.

"I live here, silly," I say, pushing hair behind my ear.

"Yeah." He closes his eyes and shakes his head, as if annoyed with me. "I know that. I meant, why did you come here tonight?"

I freeze up for a few seconds, and when I finally managed to speak, all I can say is, "Charlie told me you had a game here tonight, so I decided to come."

He sighs and glances toward the locker room door as another player comes out. "Well, thanks for coming. Hope you enjoyed it."

He steps to the side, but I grab his forearm. "Vanya, please! I came here because I wanted to talk, to apologize."

I don't exactly know how I expected him to react to me saying that, but I didn't expect him to keep mute. Instead of speaking, he looks at my hand before lifting his eyes to mine.

"Am I keeping you? Do you need to go with the team?" I point to his teammates who keep filing out of the room and walking down the long hallway, presumably toward the bus. I had to say something to distract him away from the staring contest. Looking into his eyes makes me feel guilty about the things I said to him the last time we saw each other.

"I can meet up with them later." He clears his throat and pulls his trench coat closed. "You said you wanted to talk?" he asks. "Must be important for you to track me down at work."

His joke eases some of the tension between us, and it makes me smile.

"Should we head back to your hotel then?"

"Let's take a cab. It's a cold night," he replies, putting his hand on the small of my back and leading me through the hallway.

9

KATYA

His hotel isn't far, but it would have been a twenty-minute walk, so I'm glad he suggested taking a cab. Though, the small talk on the ride was a bit awkward. I held my tongue, not wanting to spill my heart out to him in a cab.

We got to the hotel about 10 minutes later just as he predicted. It starts to drizzle as we exit the cab, so we jog to the door. His hotel room is big and spacious, with two queen beds and bright, white dressers.

"Can I get you anything? A drink? Water?" he asks.

"No, I'm good." I'm sitting on his bed with my hands in my lap, twisting my fingers nervously. My heart beats fast as I think about what to say, how to start it, how he'll respond after how I acted in New York.

"I'm going to change quickly." He nods toward the bathroom as if asking permission.

"Of course. I'll be right here," I say, patting the bed.

He grabs some clothes out of a suitcase and slips into the bathroom. He's only been in there a few seconds when my eyes dart to the door. For some reason, I have an overwhelming desire to get rid of all this awkwardness by shoving him into the shower and lathering up his naked body. We can say everything we need to say while letting the warm water run over us as our hands run over each other.

I should be thinking of what I would tell him first, not creating a bathroom fantasy in my head. I'm nervous and excited at the same time, a weird, heart-pounding mix of both.

As nervous as I am about talking to him, and apologizing to him, I'm grateful to be in his room, on his bed. When I look around the room, I catch a glance of myself in the mirror above the dresser.

"Oh God!" I snatch the beanie off my head and fluff my hair a few times, rubbing my roots with my fingertips to give it a little volume. I'm still primping when the bathroom door opens.

"Hope you didn't miss me too much." He flashes me a small smile as he enters the room again. He changed into a white T-shirt that shows off every single ripple of muscle underneath and a pair of black shorts.

"I always miss you, Vanya," I reply.

He sits beside me on the edge of the bed, my nose catching a hint of mint, as I feel his weight push the bed in. "You went out of your way to see me. What did you want to talk about?"

I've avoided eye contact, but with him sitting right there beside me, it's no longer possible. When I look into his eyes, I see questions, questions only I have the answer to. I open my mouth to speak, but the words are stuck. I've never been so nervous to talk to someone in my life.

"I—we—" I pause to gather my thoughts. It shouldn't be this hard to apologize. "The last time we saw each other, I told you that we couldn't be together. And, I gave you the wrong reasons."

"What? I'm sorry, I'm not following." He's confused, just as I expected him to be.

"When the papers said all those things about us, and I told you that we couldn't be together because of noise from the media. That it could affect our careers—" I say the words in one breath. I pause, then look up to face him again. My heart thumps so fast and hard, I'm sure he can hear it. "I lied to you. I lied to myself."

"How did you lie?"

I squeeze my eyes shut and take a deep breath. "The reason I said we couldn't be together was because I was scared. I've never felt this way for anyone before. I thought I felt something with Zhenya, but what I feel for you goes a million times beyond that, it's much deeper." I'm on a roll, connecting thoughts to words properly now. Probably because it's coming straight from my heart, with no holds barred.

"I understand, Sunshine. I've never felt like this for anyone, either," he says gently, moving closer to me on the bed and taking my hand in his. "I know you're scared, and this is going to take effort on both of our parts; but, I told you I'm willing to give it a chance if you are."

"It's going to take a lot, Vanya," I say pensively. Then I put my other hand on top of his and smile. "But we're used to that, right? Crazy schedules? Making time for things that we really want?"

"Nothing worth anything in this life comes easy. We both know that. I'm willing to give you my all." There's genuine sincerity and excitement in his words. His gaze captures mine. "I want you, Katya."

He lifts his hand to my face and caresses my cheek, moving even closer, so our thighs are flush against each other's. His eyes aren't questioning anymore, they're demanding.

I bite my lip in anticipation of what's to come.

"I want you, too," I whisper, bringing my hands to his face. "I want you, Vanya."

I can feel the passion radiating in the room. I've dreamed of this moment longer than he has—as my crush on him started well before he ever knew who I was.

I close my eyes just as his lips touch mine. My body comes alive, humming as he draws me into his arms, closing the gap between us. The kiss isn't like any we've ever shared. No, this one is much better. The last time we were just two people kissing, one of us unsure about what she wanted. But this time, we're two hearts aligned. Two people who know what they want and are ready to go for it.

I moan softly as our bodies play an erotic game of push and pull as his hands start sliding down my body. His tongue finds its way into my mouth, clashing with mine once, twice, curling, tugging, until I've gotten a proper taste of him and realize I'll never have enough.

The passion gets deeper, swirling through my body, sending pulses between my legs as it takes control. His hands slide across my back, my arms, pulling me onto his lap. The pressure intensifies, kisses get harder and deeper, creating a rhythm I enjoy. His tongue lashes mine with an urgent need I've never experienced before.

Vanya doesn't stop exploring, his hands slipping underneath my sweater, and lifting until he's easing it off. My body shudders, and my heart races. I knew from the moment our lips touched that we weren't going to stop tonight. I lean into him, yearning for the next step.

When he lifts his lips from mine, I almost protest, but then I feel his warm breath on my collarbone before his lips finally descend.

"Oh Vanya," I moan, tilting my head to one side, giving him room to explore. His tongue flicks out, teasing as he moves down, his lips grazing the valley between my breasts. I bite into my lower lip as pure pleasure travels up and down the length of my spine.

Then, his warm hands slide over the bare skin of my stomach, and he slips his thumbs underneath the soft fabric of my bra as he kisses my neck. His touch sets me on fire, leaving a trail of heat as he explores. Slowly, he moves from the small of my back until his fingers hover at the clasp of my bra. He pauses to look into my eyes. His are filled with lust and hunger—and it's all for me. He takes my mouth again with a renewed passion. I match his intensity as I return the kiss.

Vanya unclips my bra, then slides the straps off my shoulders easily. My breasts spill out, nipples taut with excitement. He lifts his mouth, licking his bottom lip as he lowers his gaze to my breasts. He takes one in his hand, his fingers grazing it before giving it a gentle squeeze.

"You're so beautiful," he says before leaning in and placing his mouth over the other. I throw my head back, my hand cupping the back of his head as I moan. He sucks on one nipple, his tongue circling the erect tip as his hand continues to fondle the other. When he switches sides, I gasp.

He stops and stands up, his gaze holding mine captive again as he slowly removes that sexy white T-shirt he has on. My breath flutters watching his smooth muscles crunch as he leans over and pulls down his shorts. My breath catches. His body could be on the cover of any fitness magazine. Over the last few weeks, I've dreamed about this moment, finally getting to touch each roll and ridge of muscle that lines his torso.

When he slides down his underwear, my eyes widen with excitement as I see him completely naked—and extremely excited—for the first time. His cock is thick and hard, encouraging the pulsating arousal that makes me so wet, I feel the gush between my legs.

He pushes me gently, and I fall onto my back with a laugh. He pulls off my boots, then removes the jeans I had on. They're off in a matter of seconds, and a couple seconds later, my damp panties with them.

"Are you sure you want this?" he asks, holding his cock, eyes searching mine as he moves closer.

"I've never been so sure of anything," I whisper. "I want you deep inside me, Vanya."

Choosing to give my body to him is an important decision. I wouldn't have turned back for anything, but I'm touched he asked. It reassures me that he cares about me and not just getting in my pants. Plus, it gives me the chance to let him know how much I want this—how much I want him.

His eyes were still searching mine, his gaze holding mine captive as he spread my legs and positioned himself at my core.

"Oh my god," I hiss with absolute satisfaction as he slowly plunges into me. He starts slowly, entering me a bit at a time with each slow thrust. The anticipation has me lifting my hips off the bed, moaning, and begging for him to enter. Then he plunges in, a swift thrust that fills me up and stretches me out completely. I wrap my legs around him as we become one, my ankles digging into the defined muscles at the back of his thighs as he starts thrusting harder.

I can't stop moaning as we make love, each thrust better than the last. The passion takes control, driving out our lust and deepest desires. He was slow and gentle at first, just gliding in and out, shifting his weight expertly on me as I felt his strokes deeper and deeper inside me. He didn't rush it, he actually knew what he was doing. He creates a rhythm for him, giving me time to get used to his size. Once I'm matching his rhythm with him, we climb higher and higher from there.

Soon, we're moving faster, my panting too getting louder. Our wet bodies slam into each other, sweat and sound our aroused bodies sweating. His panting and my moaning resonate in the huge hotel room.

"Oh, oh, Vanya," I whisper, as he goes in even deeper, my nails digging into his strong back as I hang on for support.

He thrusts faster now, while I throw my hips back and forth in an attempt to match him thrust for thrust. It goes on for a while, building and building until he pauses and swallows hard.

"I'm so close, Katya. But I want you to come, too."

I grab his hand and place it on my clit, saying, "I need stimulation here."

He nods and presses his pelvic bone against me, in the perfect spot. Then he circles and rubs, creating the friction I need. I'm already so aroused, it doesn't take long before I'm ready to sing.

"Yes, yes, yes!" I cry out, so close to succumbing to him completely, the pleasure so intense I couldn't even think straight.

He was going really hard now, it's as if his body has come alive, and with the intensity of his circling, it's only a matter of time before I hit my peak. I can feel it already, building up deep within my stomach, threatening to take hold of me at moment. We're driving recklessly close to the edge, and it's only a matter of time before we both go over.

I let out a loud moan as I hit my peak. My heart pumps faster, my thighs trembling uncontrollably as I jerk forward a few times. He hits his peak with me, low groans escaping his lips as his warmth fills me up. He pulses inside me before going completely still.

Without exchanging any words, he opens his arms, and I burrow into them. He strokes my hair until his breath returns to normal. We lay together, exhausted and satiated, enjoying the silence. Then, he pulls the comforter over us, both of us surrendering into the hands of sleep, the thoughts of the moment we just shared playing over and over in my head until I closed my eyes.

10

KATYA

I move through my hotel room, dancing around and humming a tune my father used to sing all the time as I roll my clothes and place them in my suitcase.

I have a quick meeting with Sierra, a makeup manufacturer based here in New York, to finalize the promotion for a new fragrance. After that, Charlie and I are headed to the airport for some much-needed rest and relaxation. I'm going to Detroit to be with Vanya, and Charlie is heading home to Florida. He certainly deserves it for as much travel I've subjected him to recently. He's a saint for what he allows me to do

I'm so excited to have days with Vanya at his house. We'll be together in a "normal" environment for the first time since we started seeing each other. Don't get me wrong, I love traveling and meeting up for sexy rendezvous in cities all over the country, but it can be exhausting.

Sometimes I just want to lay in bed with him making love and cuddling for an entire day without either one of us having anything else to do. But that's never the case.

Vanya is picking me up at the airport tonight when my flight gets in. I'm so excited to see him—yearning to have his lips all over me. I don't even think I'll be able to make it back to his house before I jump his bones.

I'm nearly done arranging my clothes when there's a knock on the door.

"Come on in, Charlie. The door is unlocked," I call. When he slips in, I look up. "You're early."

He quietly shuts the door behind him. "You've got an important meeting before the flight. I don't want you to be late."

"If you're here to grill me about packing, you don't have to worry. I'm already finished." I zip my suitcase, then pat it before lifting my hands over my head in a raise-the-roof celebration.

Normally, I wait until the very last minute to pack my things, which meant we had to rush to the airport so we wouldn't miss our flight. I don't know why I did it, other than it was a bad habit. Charlie tried everything to get me on track. He even went so far as to adjust the clock in my hotel room ahead by an hour. But it didn't work. In fact, the only thing that's worked has been my relationship with Vanya. Ever since we started dating, I've been extra early, eager to get to the airport and get on the plane. Because that meant I'd be in his arms soon.

"No, at all," he replies, giving me a small smile. I'd seen that smile before. He has something on his mind, something he's not sure I'll want to know.

"What is it Charlie? Do you have something to tell me?" I shove a water bottle into the oversized Louis Vuitton bag I use as a carry-on when I fly.

"Well, it's just—" He clears his throat. "When I went to check out, the concierge asked me to give this to you." He dips his hand into the pocket of his sky-blue pants and pulls out an envelope.

"What is it?" I ask, glancing at him.

"Opening your mail isn't in my job description, Katya," he deadpans, holding the envelope out to me.

"Well, that's good news." I laugh and wiggle my eyebrows at him.

I take the envelope from his hand and rip it open, removing the small card inside. As I read through the words written on it, my smile disappears.

"No, Charlie. No, no, no," I repeat, shaking my head and bringing my fingertips to my lips. It's almost as if I'm pleading with him when he doesn't even know what's on the card.

It's an invitation to a pop-up release party for my new fragrance—today at four p.m. I've been working with Sierra for over a year while the perfume has been in development. During that time, I've had input on the scent and I've done multiple print and commercial advertising photo shoots, so they have the marketing campaign ready to go.

My agent told me today's meeting was to finalize the campaign and get me the dates for future promotional events. Having to be at a release party completely blindsided me. I've got just over an hour to get there, do my makeup, and–what the hell am I going to wear?

I toss the card on the bed and quickly move to the bedside table, lifting the receiver, and punching my agent's phone number with such force, I may break a nail. After multiple rings, the call goes to her answering machine. I slam the phone down.

"Jill isn't answering." I rub the bridge of my nose with my fingers, willing the tears to stay back. I can't be red-eyed and puffy for my meeting—er, release party. "She better be at this event."

"Four o'clock," he says, letting out a deep breath as he reads the card. He sits on the edge of the bed next to my suitcase. "That's the same time as your flight."

"Yes. And Vanya is supposed to pick me up from the airport at six."

"Don't worry. We can reschedule your flight." The words roll off his lips with ease as if he's got it all figured out.

I lift my eyes to his, as hope fills my heart. "Is it that easy? To reschedule a flight?"

"Yes." He shrugs. "I mean, if they have room on a later flight it should be easy. Expensive, but easy."

I roll my eyes. "Money takes care of everything, right?"

"The event shouldn't take more than two hours. You could probably catch a nine o'clock flight if they have one."

I've always loved Charlie's optimism. It reminds me of Vanya. They both believe we can make anything work. They figure out solutions to problems instead of wallowing over them.

Sometimes, I wallow—but only for a moment.

I reach up and pull my high ponytail tighter, pacing the room while contemplating my choices. My anxiety has gone from zero to sixty in less than thirty seconds, thanks to one tiny envelope.

"I can't cancel my appearance at the event, can I?" I ask. "Tell them I didn't realize the meeting was a release party and I already had a flight scheduled?" I move closer to him, looking at him with wide, hopeful eyes. "It's the truth," I add.

"I don't think it's a good idea." He shakes his head.

I sigh in frustration and flop onto the bed. I didn't expect him to go along with it, but being shot down is still disappointing.

"You signed a contract, Katya. On top of that, I don't think it would look very good for you not to show up at the release party for a fragrance you're the face of, do you?"

"I know. I know." I look up to the ceiling.

One of the clauses in the contract is to be present at every social event surrounding the product. I just wish they would have given me a heads up. How did communication about something so important fall through the cracks? I'm going to have to talk to my agent—and her assistant.

My gaze shifts from the ceiling to the clock, and I realize how late it is. I jump off the bed. "Shit! Charlie, I've got to get to the Sierra offices." I grab the handle of my suitcase and set it on the floor. "Let's go!"

"You should call Vanya and tell him what happened." He points to the telephone. "Tell him you'll be taking the later flight instead, ask if he can still pick you up."

"Yes! Of course!" I nod and race to the telephone again. When I dial his number, there's a busy signal. I hang up and try again. Same thing.

"I keep getting a busy signal." To lighten the mood—my mood—I joke, "Shouldn't Vanya know to keep his line open at all times for my call?"

When I turn around, Charlie is right behind me. He places a hand on my shoulder. "You can try him again later. It's almost noon, and if you want to be ready for that party, you've gotta get your ass in a cab and high-tail it to Sierra. And I need to get to the airport."

"Wait. You're not going with me to the party?" I ask. Charlie and I go everywhere together. He's a star in the tennis world and recently well known in fashion circles since he's been by my side since I was fifteen.

"You're eighteen-years-old, Katya. You don't need a chaperone anymore."

"Is that what you've been? A chaperone for an underage tennis player?"

"We can talk about this in the elevator."

"You're right," I say, pulling up the handle on my suitcase and rolling it toward the door.

"You were ready on time and you're still going to make me late," Charlie teases as we exit my room and walk through the hallway.

I laugh. "Some things never, change, yes?"

As disappointed as I am of not being able to hop on the early flight, I really am excited about this fragrance. Plus, it's all part of the job—the part of the job I love.

"I really hope they have hair and makeup ready and waiting—and a dress." I turn to Charlie, suddenly panicked. "I have nothing. Should we stop by a department store?"

"Relax, Katya." He slides his arm across my shoulders. "You've done this a thousand times. I'm sure they'll have an outfit picked out for you and a rack of designer clothing on standby in case you don't like it."

I nod, knowing he's right. My brain is working overtime from stress.

"Did you decide? Are you going with me?" I ask just before he opens the door to exit the hotel.

"Of course, Katya. We go everywhere together," he replies and flashes me a bright smile. Then he rushes to the curb to hail a cab.

* * *

As soon as I get to Sierra, I'm ushered through the main offices and into a conference room where my agent is siting.

"Katya!" She stands up and moves to me, taking me in her arms. "I'm so glad you made it."

"Jill, what's going on? I thought this was a meeting to finalize—" I start on my rampage, but she grabs my shoulders and looks me in the eyes.

"Take a deep breath."

I do as she says, and she lets my shoulders go.

"There was a huge mix up with my new assistant. I just hired her and training has been slower than I expected."

"That's not my problem," I tell her crossing my arms. Being a bitch isn't my style, but at the same time, I'm a client and this was a big mess up. Adapt and assimilate are my middle name, but I'll speak my mind when necessary.

"Do you have your cell phone?"

"No, the battery is dead and won't charge, so I left it home. I planned on getting a new one this week."

"So that's why you never answered," Jill says. "She left multiple messages on your cell."

Heat rises in my cheeks. "Are you saying this is my fault?" I ask, indignantly. "Because your staff knows I stay at the Castle every time I'm in New York, and they could have easily called my room or the front desk."

She puts her hands over her heart. "Katya, I take full responsibility. If my team fucks up, it's my fuck up, and I'm sorry. Can we move forward and get you to hair and makeup?"

I close my eyes and take another deep breath, willing myself to put everything in perspective. Mistakes happen. The only reason I'm this upset about it is because I was supposed to meet Vanya. Any other day I'd be happy to have another party to attend.

"Yes," I say calmly, allowing her to lead me through a hallway to a large room filled with hair and clothing stylists and makeup artists. Time to relax and let the professionals work their magic.

* * *

I'D HOPED the event would start promptly at four, but in true New York party style, it's 4:30 p.m., and people are still sailing through the doors of Rudson's department store.

"Four o'clock my ass," I mumble to Charlie while still keeping a smile plastered on my face. A woman who seems to know me waves from across the room. I return the gesture, though I don't recognize her at all.

"Relax and try to enjoy the moment," he replies as he adjusts the button of his suitcoat. "You look stunning, by the way."

I blush. The short, red cocktail dress the stylist picked out fits me perfectly, and it's so comfortable it could be a nightgown.

"You don't look too bad yourself," I tell him, bumping his arm with my elbow. "I love the way they gelled your hair off your forehead. It brings out your features."

I reach out to touch it, but he bats my hand away with catlike reflexes, which makes me giggle.

"My, aren't we vain tonight," I tease, which earns me a big laugh. Charlie would much rather be in a polo and shorts, but he suffers for me.

I catch sight of a three-tiered-tray of multi-colored macaroons on a dessert table across the room and wonder when I'll be able to sneak over there.

"Stop fidgeting, Katya," Charlie says.

"I'm restless, Charlie. I really want to see Vanya tonight," I whine.

Just then, a waiter carrying a tray of champagne walks by, Charlie stops him and takes two glasses.

"Here, drink," he commands, handing me a glass. "And for the love of god, relax. If you look too shifty, people will think you're on drugs."

I slap his shoulder playfully. "Stop!"

He laughs, bringing a bubbling glass of champagne to his lips. "Once the fragrance is revealed, you can make a graceful exit."

Just as I'm sipping my first glass, Jill whisks me away from Charlie. There's no shortage of people who want to meet me, shake my hand, take a photo, or talk about tennis. As one of the youngest, if not actually the youngest tennis champion in history, everyone wants to hear my story.

I'm not sure how long Jill has been zipping me around the room, but if I measure it in drinks, I've had three glasses of champagne and zero water. I'm starting to feel a little tipsy, but overall, I'm good. She hands me a glass of water and rushes me to the front of the room while someone from Sierra steps up to the microphone and directs everyone's attention to the stage to hear Andres Martinez, Latin King of Pop, perform his latest single.

I've heard Andres' music and love it, but I've never had the chance to attend one of his shows. I sip my water and watch as his band starts playing behind him. His eyes are closed as he grips the microphone and stands tall in a vintage gray t-shirt and dark, blue jeans. When he starts singing, he opens his eyes and looks at me. Well, not me in particular, but he looked out at the crowd and I happen to be front row.

There's no doubt in my mind why Andres was named sexiest man alive last year by multiple magazines. He's absolutely mouth-watering with his dark hair, smoldering eyes, and muscular brown skin. He has the most sultry singing voice—in Spanish and English—which he switches between during the song.

I have to remind myself not to stare, but he has that all-consuming charisma lead singers have. I may need a cold shower after this one.

When Andres is finished I let out a breath, Sandra Latham, Director of Product Development at Sierra, walks up to the microphone stand located next to a white wall covered with a black curtain.

"Ladies and gentlemen, I'd like to thank everyone for being here for the grand reveal of our newest fragrance. We at Sierra are so grateful to Katya Novikova, two-time tennis Grand Slam champion, for signing on to be the face of this fragrance. Thank you, Katya, for giving us so much of your time and for working tirelessly on this project." Sandra stops and holds her arms out. I step into them, embracing her as the crowd applauds.

She releases me and continues, "When we set out to create this fragrance, we were so inspired by Katya. We wanted to capture her essence in a scent. We needed something fresh and sexy. Sporty yet feminine. Graceful, but strong. And so, without further ado, I'm proud to introduce, Katya by Sierra!"

As soon as she finishes, the curtain drops, revealing a huge poster of me in a white tennis dress next to a net at center court. The fragrance sits in the bottom right. I heard her say my name, but I didn't quite understand until I read the bold type on the top of the advertisement. "Katya" by Sierra.

"Katya" is the name of the fragrance.

I'm so struck by surprise, my knees almost buckle. My heart races, and my knees shake as I turn around and throw my arms around Sandra again.

"I had no idea!" I tell her.

"Now you see why we wanted this pop up to be a surprise for you."

"It's amazing. Thank you!"

Once the initial surprise wears off, I flip the nervous energy into playing it up for the crowd. I stand in front of the poster, smiling brightly as flashbulbs go off every few seconds.

Sandra, who's still at the microphone, clears her throat. "Katya has a huge heart and is very involved with charities. Knowing that, and wanting to capture her generous spirit, we decided that a portion of the proceeds of this fragrance will go to a national network of children's hospitals who provide free medical care for patients." She pauses, allowing the crowd to cheer and applaud again. "So, please, eat, drink, enjoy! Let's celebrate a wonderful woman and this wonderful moment."

I can't believe my ears. Tying the product to any of the charities I work with wasn't something I knew about at all. In casual conversation, people at Sierra had asked me questions about organizations, but they never went into depth. I didn't think anything of it.

It's absolutely amazing to have this moment. When Sandra steps away from the podium, I hug her again. She's probably going to file a restraining order on me, but I can't help it. I'm so overwhelmed by emotion.

After shaking hands and thanking a line of people from Sierra with Jill at my side, she pulls me away to mix and mingle again. Thankfully, she takes me to a group where Charlie has been chatting happily.

"Congratulations, my dear," he kisses me on the cheeks.

"It's amazing, isn't it?" I spin around, taking in every sight and sound of the party. I stumble a bit when I turn back to him. "Charlie, I had no idea!"

"It's a very special moment. Enjoy it." He takes the drink from my hand and replaces it with water. I appreciate that he looks out for me. I didn't how much alcohol I'd had in a short period of time.

I've only been talking to Charlie for a moment, when suddenly, Jill barrels back in and grabs my arm. I hadn't even realized she left.

"You will never guess who I just talked to," she says.

"Who?" I'm hanging on every word.

"Andres Martinez's agent," she responds. "Andres wants you to be in his next video."

"What?" I shake my head in disbelief. "Me?"

"Yes. Are you interested?"

"Am I interested? Of course!" I hop up, which isn't a good idea in five-inch heels, as I waver a bit. Charlie holds my arm to steady me.

"I thought you'd say that. We exchanged numbers. I'll figure out the details and run it by as soon as I know what's going on," she says. She touches my shoulder. "Honey, you have been such a rock star tonight. Let's go say goodbye to the Sierra folks and get you and Charlie in a cab."

* * *

"Charlie, I'm never going to m-make it on a flight." I say, trying to stand upright, but my wobbly legs know Charlie's doing most of the work.

"Don't worry, Katya. We missed that flight, anyway."

"Vanya. What about—" I lean forward, until my forehead hits the door. "I think I'm going to be sick."

"Hold on, now," he says, unlocking the door and ushering me inside. He leads me straight to the bathroom. Immediately, my legs buckle and I crumple onto the floor next to the toilet. I lean my elbow on the rim and prop up my head.

"Katya," he scolds, gathering my hair in his hands and securing it with an elastic band.

"I know, I know." I wave him off, and lay my cheek down on the rim of the bowl. The cold porcelain feels good on my flushed face.

"Do you need me to stay?" he winces as if it's the last thing he wants to do. I don't blame him. The smell of vomit makes me sick, so I never hang around when someone else is doing it.

"I'm okay."

He leaves the room for a moment, and comes back with a glass of ice, which he sets on the floor next to me. "It might help to chew on those. I'll check on you in the morning."

"Charlie!" I call out meekly, barely able to find my voice. When he turns, I continue, "Thank you."

"Get some rest, Katya."

* * *

When I wake up, I'm lying on the bathroom floor with a fluffy white towel pulled over me like a blanket. My hand flies to my pounding forehead, as I sit up. Slowly, I reach forward and start crawling. The hotel room is completely dark, but I find my way to the bed, climb into it, and curl up under the covers.

Before I close my eyes, I pop my head out and check the time. 3:27 a.m.

I missed my flight to Detroit last night, missed the chance to get to Vanya, and had far too much champagne. I groan and bury my head again before drifting off.

"Katya!" Charlie pounds on my door seconds later.

Well, it felt like seconds, but when I throw the blanket off my head, a glance at the clock tells me it's ten after seven.

"Katya! You've gotta to get up. You've got a flight to Detroit at ten."

His announcement makes me scramble out of bed. I'm still wearing last night's dress, and probably have last night's eye makeup running down my cheeks. I rush to the door and let him in.

"Your bag is packed from yesterday, right?" Charlie asks, kindly ignoring my appearance as he sets a cup of coffee on my dresser.

I nod.

"Jump in the shower. We've got to get a move on."

Without delay, I hightail it to the bathroom, and take the fastest shower ever.

11

VANYA

"Katya," I whisper, smiling and pushing her head toward my cock. I tense in anticipation as her warm breath sends chills through me. Just as she's about to cover me with her mouth, a loud, annoying buzzing fills the air.

My eyes pop open and I realize I'm alone in my bed holding a pillow over my dick. The alarm blares in my ear, until I reach over and slap it. Normally, I never press snooze, but I really want to get back into that dream. Especially being interrupted at such a pivotal moment.

But my body is so used to waking up at the same time almost every day, it doesn't allow me to fall back asleep.

Out of all the things that quickly run through my head, it's the thought of her that lingers. Since I have a minute, I lean over and grab the latest issue of MX men's magazine, where my girlfriend graces the cover in nothing but a black leather bikini. If I can't have her in my dreams, I can rub one out while looking at her—like millions of other men around the world. It doesn't bother me. In fact, it turns me on even more. One of the most lusted after women in the world is mine.

I turn to the center, where there's a photo of her kneeing on the beach, legs spread with one hand behind her head, and the other with her thumb hooked into the front of the practically non-existent swim suit pulling it down slightly in front. She's wet, with her blonde hair slicked back and sand glittering on her bronzed skin.

I spit in my hand and grab hold of my cock, imagining my face between her legs, mouth directly over the prized spot. With every lick, I rub my cock up and down which feels amazing in my current state. I allow myself to drift into the moment, remembering how soft her skin felt under my fingers and her intoxicating scent. There's no stopping now. I'm licking, sucking, lapping at her, making sure I coat every inch of my tongue in her juices.

The thought of her cum dripping off my chin is what brings me to my peak. My cock throbs and pulses in my hand, and I swear I see stars when I squirt. I drop the magazine, saying, "Oh yes! Fuck yes!" through an exhale.

The release is absolute ecstasy. Though, I'd rather be doing it inside Katya than on my bed.

I let myself enjoy the moment, zoning out and catching my breath before squeezing out every last drop.

I add changing and washing my sheets to the list of things I have to do today before I pick Katya up from the airport tonight. She's spending a few days with me in Detroit and I couldn't be more excited. The Chargers have a three-game home stand, so I'm home for over a week, which rarely happens.

The last few months feel like I've been living in a dream—which is how I expect life with Katya will always be as long as we're both working. Our relationship has felt like a series of mini-vacations since we've been together. Imagine getting to have all your dates in different cities across the US and Canada? That's gotta go down as one of the coolest courtships in dating history. But we do what we have to in order to see each other when we can.

Katya usually travels to where I am, because I don't have many free days in my schedule. She doesn't either, but she can train from whatever city she's in, while I have to stay with my team.

I never expected her to show up after my game in Florida. I knew she lived in Miami, but I didn't expect her to visit. Not after how we'd left things in New York.

I thought about calling her a million times over the month we didn't communicate. But I wanted to give her space. Plus, I don't believe in chasing women. Pursuing them? Yes. But chasing after she's told me she's not interested? No. If she doesn't want to be with me, I respect the decision, no matter how much it might sting.

I don't have time for any more games than the eighty already on my schedule.

Not to say I won't give someone another chance. I know Katya is young and scared. She's affected by what the press reports. Their stories—truth or not—weigh on her heavily, rightfully so as they've turned her into a sex symbol and marketing machine. I don't understand how she can even focus on her tennis career with what she has to put up with.

But I knew, if she was going to come back to me, she'd wait until after she'd turned eighteen.

Maybe that's what was going through my subconscious when I sent a massive bouquet of roses to her home for her birthday.

* * *

I SPENT LONGER than usual in front of the mirror checking my freshly-shaved face to see if I missed any spots. When I'm satisfied with my look, I get dressed. I check the time as I strap on my silver Tag Heuer. It'll only take me twenty minutes to get to the airport, but I want to stop and get Katya something on the way.

By five fifteen, I'm in my Mercedes heading to the only flower shop I know of, a local place not far from my house. I've never been in there, only passed it, but it'll serve the purpose.

Upon opening the door of the dimly lit store, I see multiple people mulling around, sniffing flowers or running their fingers along them. When I step in, various pungent scents assault my nose, making me feel slightly sick for a moment. I stand there, taking a second to let the nausea pass, when a woman calls out to me.

"You need help or are you just gonna stand there?" Her accent is thick, but I can't tell what nationality. It's definitely not Eastern European. Maybe Spanish or Italian?

A few people look up, but most keep their head down, which means they don't want to embarrass me, or this woman is like this all the time and it's not something to bat an eyelash at. I'll bet my car it's the latter.

"I look at these flowers for my girlfriend," I reply, remembering to smile, as Americans do.

"What's your girlfriend's favorite kind of flower?" she asks, showing a set of tobacco-stained teeth while she speaks.

"No clue," I say, running my fingers through my dark blond hair knowing this lady's not going to be happy about my answer.

"What kind of man doesn't know his girlfriend's favorite flower?" She gives me a disgusted look, as if she just wiped me off the bottom of her shoe.

"We just start dating. This I do not know." I keep my cool. A crotchety old lady in a flower shop isn't going to make me blink twice. I actually like her. Her direct demeanor reminds me of old woman back home.

She pauses, sizing me up from underneath thick dark eyebrows. At first, I think she's going to kick me out of the shop empty-handed. Still, I stand my ground, showing I'm unaffected by her scrutiny.

"Alright, follow me," she finally says and leads me to a different section of the store. "Don't suppose you know her favorite color either, eh?" she asks as we stop in front of a wall of flowers, all grouped together in large buckets.

"Nope," I tell her, shaking my head and crossing my arms over my chest. I haven't asked a woman what her favorite color was since I was in primary school.

"I like you," she says abruptly, which surprises the shit out of me. "I'll pick you something she'll love."

She smiles then rubs her forefinger over her chin as she scans the wall of flowers. "I've been selling flowers for over forty years. Right here in this store." She points to the ground. I follow her finger as if there's a historical marker under her feet. "I can tell you what every flower symbolizes."

"Red roses do not work for every time?"

She rubs her lower back as if it's stiff, while dismissing a bucket of red roses with a wave of her other hand. "Red roses are beautiful, but cliché."

"I think they are love, yes?"

"Yes. Boring, plain old love."

The woman moves to the next bucket and plucks out a yellow rose. She brings it to her nose, closes her eyes, and inhales before returning it. Yellow roses are a symbol of friendship."

I watch closely as she handles the flowers. She loves this—both the flowers and a captive audience. I appreciate that because I love a captive audience when I'm doing what I do best as well.

She stops in front of another red flower, *krasnyy tyul'pan* in my language.

"But red tulips!" She lifts one of them and brings it to her nose as she did the yellow rose. "Red tulips symbolize passion. And that's what I see in you." She winks as if we've shared a special moment. "Give her these," she says, grabbing a new bundle and shoving the flowers at me.

I accept the bouquet and count them quickly. Twelve beautiful red tulips. "I need twenty-three of these."

"What are you, a wise guy?" she asks, tilting her head as if I'm playing a joke on her. A joke she's not amused with.

"Is my tradition to give odd number."

The woman folds her arms across her chest. "Where?"

"In Russia. We only give even number flowers at funerals."

"Really?"

I nod.

"I guess we both learned something today," she says, smiling as she hands me the bouquet where she'd removed a flower to smell, making it a bundle of eleven. "Head to the front and my daughter will check you out."

"Thank you for your help. I appreciate this." I smile back as I collect the flowers.

* * *

I ARRIVE at the airport at exactly 5:45 p.m., fifteen minutes before Katya is scheduled to land. I wait outside the gate where her flight is due, shifting on my feet as I look out the window. When I see the plane pull up to the gate, I can't help but smile. I can't wait to hold her in my arms and bring her to my bed.

Waiting for people to deplane seems to take forever. I watch with baited breath as passengers exit. There's a large group, then a gap, followed by more people. I thought Katya traveled first class and would have been one of the first people off the plane, but she's not in any of the early groups.

When she still doesn't come through the door with the last stragglers, I can't help but wonder if I got the flight time wrong. Maybe she departed at 6:00 p.m. instead of arriving at that time. My thoughts have been so scattered recently trying to remember her schedule and my schedule that I totally could have made that mistake.

I rush to the agent at the gate and ask if there's anyone left on the plane.

"I'm sorry, sir. It's empty. They're cleaning it for the next flight out."

I shift the flowers from my right to left hand. "I'm waiting for a friend, Ekaterina Novikova. Was she on the plane?"

"Let me check the roster." She taps away on her keyboard, eyes scanning the screen quickly. Suddenly, she frowns. "Ms. Novikova was supposed to be on this flight, but she never checked in."

"Thank you."

There's a pit of fear in my stomach wondering why Katya missed her flight. I'm not usually one to worry, but it's not like her to miss time with me and not call. Then again, maybe she called while I was on my way and I missed it.

Absentmindedly, I turn around and start walking through the

concourse. When I see a group of pay phones, I stop and dig into my pocket for change. I quickly punch in the number to her mobile phone. It rings and rings, but she doesn't answer.

There's still a possibility that Katya missed her flight and is on a later plane to Detroit and calling her hotel room in New York is a waste of time, but I have to try.

I hang up, deposit more change, then call the Castle, the hotel she always stays at when she's in the City.

"Thank you for calling the Castle New York," a woman answers. "How may I help you this evening?"

"Yes, hello. This is Ivan Kravtsov. I need Ekaterina Novikova in room two-fifty-seven, please." I always tell them my name because I'm on a list of approved callers whose calls can be directed to her room.

"I'm sorry, Sir. Ms. Novikova checked out earlier today."

"Thank you," I say, hanging up before the woman can reply.

It's not like her to not let me know if her plans change. If she missed her flight, she had plenty of time to call before I left the house. I rub my eyes, tired and frustrated. The only thing to do is go back home and check my messages.

* * *

THE DRIVE home only enhanced the annoyance I already felt leaving the airport alone. What began as a light rain when I got in my car, started coming down so hard I could barely see the lights of the car in front of me. Traffic was so heavy; all the cars literally came to a standstill. Not only was it rush hour, there was also an accident. Even though the police and first responders were at the front trying to clear two of the three lanes to get things moving again, I spent almost an hour sitting there.

It's after eight when I walk through the door. The first thing I do is toss my keys on the table and rush to the answering machine, hoping there's a message from Katya. But the light isn't blinking at all. Anger seeps into every pore.

How could she do something so selfish and not even call?

Just as I turn to go to the living room, I hear a noise. It's a weird, tiny beeping sound. I glance at the answering machine, but don't see anything odd. Then, I look at the phone itself. The receiver is partially off the hook.

Shit.

The phone has been off the hook. Even if Katya tried to call, it wouldn't have gone through. I shrug off my coat, annoyed at myself. Then I trash the flowers and order a pizza. Both anger and worry subside slightly.

To clear my mind, I stretch out on the couch, pop on the T.V., and wait for the pizza to arrive.

Though I've hooked up with quite a few women, I've only had a couple girlfriends—women I've dated more than once. I forgot how edgy it made me feel when I was thinking about another person constantly. Which is probably a big reason I didn't have many girlfriends—they're a distraction.

12

VANYA

The next morning, I still haven't heard from Katya. I try her mobile phone again, but it goes right to a full voice mail box. My heart races, worried at what could have happened that she missed her flight and didn't call.

I don't have time to sit and stew because I have to be at the arena for practice. Then, I have a meeting with Brookins and my translator, Viktor "Vitya" Berezin, to sign my newest contract. After months of Kirya negotiating on my behalf, the Chargers and I finally came to an agreement—a four-year, 2.7-million-dollar contract.

I've just finished getting dressed when Novotný pops his head into the locker room and tells me my translator is waiting in the hallway. Even though I know Kirya has gone over it a million times, I always send Vitya a copy to review and ask him to join me for meetings when I'm signing documents. You can never be too careful.

"Perfect timing," I say to myself as I fasten my belt. I grab my coat, stuff my car keys in my pocket, and head to the hallway to meet him.

"Vitya," I greet the older man. He turns his head and smiles, walking toward me with his beige trench coat flapping against his calves.

"You look tired, Vanya. Have you been getting enough sleep?"

I laugh and kiss his cheeks. "Plenty. Thanks for your concern."

As we start walking toward the Assistant GM's office, Vitya leans closer and lowers his voice. "I have more concerns."

I stop abruptly, uneasy at his surprising comment. "About the contract?"

"Are you mafia, Vanya?" he asks, cutting straight to the point.

I laugh. "No. Why would you ask such a thing?" I start walking again.

"Because your agent is mafia." Vitya removes his jacket and hangs it over his arm.

Kirya's affiliations weren't something I was ever going to bring up, but my friend is a smart, connected man. I knew he would realize sooner or later. "Everyone has shady people in their life. As long as they do well by me, what can I say?"

He grabs my shoulders and holds my gaze. "Let me give you the number of a friend. He can be your agent. Leave the mafia connections behind."

I laugh. "That's going to be hard since my agent is the closest thing I have to a brother."

Viktor lifts his hands and steps back as if I'm on fire. "I had no idea."

"He's a good man. I owe him my career. I can't do anything about his ties. They have nothing to do with me."

"You are who you surround yourself with," he says in a stern voice.

I slap his shoulder. "I appreciate how you look out for me. But I've known Kirya since I was a boy. We're more brothers than friends. Without his help, I never would have gotten to America. And as my agent, he saved me from being extorted by another bratva."

"He saved you from paying another bratva because, by being your agent, he's getting money for his own to be your krysha."

As we stand outside the office talking in hushed tones, I realize I've got to shut it down. I'm not switching agents. On the contrary, I'm about to jump into business with Kirya again soon. But that's a talk for another day with my American father figure.

"I'm lucky to have you in my life, Vitya. You and Catherine have treated me like family since I've been in Detroit, and I couldn't be more grateful. Let's put this aside, get in there, and sign a multi-million-dollar contract."

He slides his arm across my shoulder and gives me a slight hug. "You deserve it, Vanya. You've worked very hard for this."

When I rap my knuckles against Brookins' office door, his thin, gold-plated name tag rattles against the heavy wood. There's no answer at first, so I knock again, slightly harder this time.

"Yeah. Come on in," he calls from inside.

I open the door and walk in before Vitya. "Hey, Brooksy. I have Viktor with me."

Brookins' head is down, sleeves rolled up, and he's scribbling furiously. Then he drops his pen and stands. "Viktor, it's nice to see you again." The men shake hands over his desk. He gestures to two empty chairs. "Have a seat, please."

While we sit down, he shoves a few papers into a manila folder and sets it on a pile of other folders. Then he grabs another one and removes the papers.

I lean forward, grabbing a black pen from a cup on the corner of his desk, excited to sign. I love playing for the Chargers organization, and I'm proud they want to invest in me and consider me the future of the team.

"You've read thorough it, correct? We had a copy translated into Russian and sent to you and your agent."

I nod.

"Do you have any questions?"

I adjust myself on the seat and throw a glance toward Vitya for confirmation that the contract looks good from his perspective. He shakes his head as if to say "no questions."

"Great. Just initial here and here, and sign here," Brookins points to different lines. He puts another piece of paper on top. "And this is for the signing bonus."

Adrenaline ripples through my veins, and my hands shake as I scratch my name. Never in a million moons did I think I'd be signing a contract for so much money.

Once we've finished the paperwork, he stacks it up, secures it with a paperclip, and slides it into another folder. "After Mr. Popovic signs, we'll send you a copy with original signatures and send a copy to your agent."

"Sounds good." My knee shakes as I sit there waiting to be dismissed as he writes something on a sticky note and pops it onto the folder.

Brookins, in particular, doesn't make me nervous. He's never made me uncomfortable, and he risked prison-time by being involved in my defection. For that, I'll always be grateful.

I'm uneasy because sitting in a hockey team's administrative office reminds me of my time with the Central Scarlet Army. The only time I was asked to report to the coach's office meant Myskin wanted was going to scream at me about something—usually something insignificant.

"So—" He clears his throat as he sets his pen down. "I saw some articles about you and a tennis player a few weeks back."

"Yes. Katya Novikova," I reply, crossing my legs to keep my knee from shaking. I know how some of my teammates feel about my relationship, but I've been riding the storm and keeping a low profile with the organization. Up until today, no one has mentioned it. "The press, they talk."

"Are you aware of what the press is saying?"

"I am aware but," I pause, trying to think of the English words I need. "I do not listen."

"Look, Ivan, your personal life is none of my business, but I will say, American press is a beast. Not the local newspapers. While, some people want to hear about the intimate details of your life, most Detroiters only care about what you're doing on the ice and if it's going to help us win a Stanley Cup." He removes his glasses and places both elbows on his huge mahogany desk. He looks tired, like he hasn't slept in days.

"It's the paparazzi types you need to watch out for. And Novikova is all the rage. She's at the top of all of their lists."

"I understand, Sir. It's something Katya and I have discussed at length."

"Like I said, I don't care about your personal life, but I do care about how it effects your play and this team."

I lean forward, confused. "Have I been, uh—" I look to Vitya to help me find the word. "Neeffektivnyye?" I ask him.

"Ineffective, underperforming," he tells me.

I know the answer before I even ask the question. I'm having the best season of my career—as evidenced by the contract I signed moments ago. The stories about Katya and I have been an annoyance, but it hasn't affected my game. I train hard. I play hard. I'm one-hundred percent focused on my career.

I look to Brookins, who heard Vitya's translation.

"No. Not at all actually." He glances around the room as if he was looking for something before finally settling on my face. "I just want to make sure it doesn't become a distraction."

"May I speak honest?" I ask.

He nods.

I turn to Vitya, and ask him to translate for me.

"I give you my word that I have never, and would never, let a relationship affect my play. I am one hundred percent committed to this team."

He nods as Vitya translate my words. "Thank you for your commitment." He stands up and stretches his hand across his desk. I rise and shake his hand. "We're excited for the future with you, Ivan. Very excited."

"Same, Sir."

Vitya and I leave Brookins' office and start down the hallway. He's sliding one arm into his coat when I ask, "Do you think it's weird that he talked to me about Katya? Is that normal?"

He looks up and shrugs. "I don't know if it's normal, but I'm sure many players get a talk when their personal life is all over the news. They're trying to protect their investment and make sure you're focused."

"There are many players—not necessarily on the Chargers—but lots of guys who are with different high-profile women all the time." I pause, thinking about all the singers, models, and actresses I've seen guys with. "It seems to me being in the public eye for dating a lot of women is just as distracting than it would be dating just one," I reply with a low chuckle.

"Vanya, everyone has personal life. And it's going to come up every once in a while. Even guys who are married. Stay focused on your game and try not to let the stress of the media get to you."

I nod. One of the best things about Vitya is that he'll always tell me the truth, which isn't always what I want to hear, but at least I know I can trust his opinion.

He claps my shoulder. "Commitment takes time, and so does hockey. Find a balance and always be honest with yourself."

* * *

When I get home from the arena, my phone is ringing. I unlock the door quickly, hoping I get to the kitchen in time to grab it.

I dash through the living room, getting to the receiver on the fifth ring. "Hello?"

"Vanya, it's me!" Katya says, her voice bright and bubbly as always.

Despite still holding onto a tinge of irritation, I breathe a sigh of relief. After not hearing from her last night, and not being able to reach her, most of the anger I had turned to fear. We hadn't gone a day without speaking to each other in weeks, and I had a feeling in the pit of my stomach that something was wrong.

"I'm so glad to hear from you, Sunshine. Are you all right? I've been worried sick."

"Yes, I'm fine. I'm so sorry, Vanya."

"What happened yesterday?"

"I'll explain everything, I promise. But I have a favor to ask first."

"A favor? I waited for you at the airport for over an hour yesterday and you have a favor to ask of me?"

"Well, now I'm the one waiting for you."

"Waiting for me? How?' I ask.

"I'm at the airport in Detroit, waiting for you to pick me up," she replies. My face instantly lights up.

"I didn't realize I was supposed to."

"That's the favor."

"Wait. You're there now?"

"Yes. My flight got in twenty minutes ago. And it'll take you about twenty minutes to get here, right?"

"Correct."

"So we're even."

I laugh. "Hold tight, Sunshine. I'm on my way," I say, hanging the receiver on the cradle before heading back to the front door.

"I can't wait to see you," she whispers.

* * *

As I pull up in front of the arrivals area at the North terminal, I find Katya right away. She's sitting on a bench outside the doors with her suitcase at her feet. I pull the car to the side, and get out quickly.

"Vanya!" she cries out when she sees me. She runs toward me and jumps into my arms. Thankfully, I'm ready for it. I'm not prepared for her to pepper my face with kisses.

"Hi, Sunshine," I say, when she lets up. I nuzzle my face in her neck and inhale her sweet powdery scent. Having Katya in my arms again feels like home. Being with her makes all my doubts wash away.

"I'm so happy to be here right now." She pulls her head back and looks at me. "I thought you'd hate me."

"I could never hate you, love." I smile, cupping her chin between my thumb and forefinger. "What happened yesterday?"

When we break apart, she blows into her hands and rubs her them together. "Can we continue this in the car? I have so much to tell you."

"Of course."

I open the passenger door and let her get in before shutting it and grabbing her suitcase. After tossing it in the trunk, I get it the car.

Our eyes meet, and I'm immediately drawn to her smile—her lips, actually. Before shifting out of park and getting on the road, I lean over and kiss her. She responds immediately, pressing her mouth to mine with urgency as her fingers weave into my hair. Blood rushes to my dick. I've got to get her to my house.

"Are you hungry?" I ask.

Her cheeks are flushed as she shakes her head.

"Good, because I can't wait to get you home." I wink, then shift into drive and check my mirrors before merging into the traffic leaving the airport. I reach over and set my hand on her thigh. She takes it in both of hers, squeezing it gently.

"Now we can talk, yes?" she asks. "Yesterday was crazy, Vanya. Crazy and wonderful."

"It must be good if you still had a wonderful day even after missing your flight to see me," I tease, smiling to make sure she knows I'm poking fun.

"Once you hear why, you'll be happy for me." She crosses her arms across her chest and sticks her tongue out at me. "I tried calling you, but I kept getting a busy signal. I called twice from the hotel. I even tried from the party."

"Yeah," I say, sheepishly, rubbing the back of my neck. "That was my fault. I guess I didn't hang the phone up all the way and it was off the receiver. I had no idea until I got home from the airport last night. I'm sorry."

"Oh no!" She laughs, leaning her head against the rest. "It's a comedy of errors with us sometimes, isn't it?"

"Right? So, go on. What party?"

"You know that fragrance I've been working on with Sierra?" she asks. When I nod, she continues. "I had a meeting scheduled to go over the final marketing promotions, but instead of a meeting, it was a pop-up release party for the fragrance."

"Really? They didn't tell you?"

"No," she exclaims. "All I got was an invitation that someone dropped off at the front desk of our hotel yesterday at noon. If Charlie hadn't gone to the desk to check out, I never would have gotten it."

"That seems odd."

"Yes! But don't worry, I talked to my agent and got it figured out. It was a huge mix-up with her new assistant who she's been training."

"So, you went to a New York party instead of catching your flight to see me? I see where I stand, Katya." I squeeze her knee.

"It wasn't just a party, Vanya. It was a surprise for me." She grabs my forearm and turns to me. "They named the fragrance Katya!" She squeals.

"You're kidding?" I ask with wide eyes. She shakes her head. "Kayta, that's amazing! You have your own perfume. That's huge!"

"Yes!"

I love the pride in her eyes and excitement in her voice. It makes my heart swell with happiness for her.

"Well, I'd say that's a fine reason to miss your flight."

"And, I didn't call last night after the party because—" Her face scrunches up and she bites her lip.

I glance at her, widening my eyes as if beckoning her to continue. "Because?" I draw the word out.

Her gaze moves to the floor. "I passed out."

I burst out laughing, which makes the wheel shake a bit, I check the mirrors and correct myself immediately.

"The champagne was flowing, Vanya!" She giggles. "And you know how much of a lightweight I am."

I reach out and touch her cheek. "I'm so proud of you."

"It was so surreal. I was actually a bit pissed when I got the invitation. Though I didn't know the surprise part of it, I wondered how something so important as a release party had slipped through the cracks."

"That's understandable, though. I mean, you have a busy life. A slip like that is massive."

"Are you okay." Her brows furrow with concern as she reaches out and traces the skin under my eye with her thumb. "You look stressed."

"I'm good. I swear." I grab her hand and kiss it. "I actually have good news, too."

"Really?" She tucks one leg under her butt and turns toward me. "What is it?"

"I signed a contract extension this morning." I glance at her quickly. "The Chargers want me for four more years."

"That's wonderful! They see you as their future."

"Can you handle four more years in Detroit?" As soon as I say it, I realize how presumptuous it sounds. We've barely been dating for two months and I'm asking her about the next four years.

I shake my head. "Forget I said that."

"I'll go anywhere you are, Vanya. I love you."

The words surprise me, but a jolt of adrenaline hits me as I process them. "I know I said we were going directly home, but do you mind if we make one quick stop first?"

"Not at all."

We laugh and chat happily as we drive. She tells me about the party and how she smiled so much her face hurt.

"I thought that only happened when you were with me?" I ask, feigning being offended. "We're here," I announce just before I swing the car into a parking spot.

"A flower shop?" she asks as she scrambles out of the car. When I round the corner, I grab her hand, and she kisses me.

Upon entering, I have my eyes peeled for the old woman who helped me pick flowers the day before, but I don't see her. I lead Katya to the back wall, watching with a smile as her face lights up.

"What are your favorite flowers?" I ask.

"Tulips," she replies, walking down a bit, and pulling a bouquet out.

"I bought tulips for you yesterday. An older lady I met here advised me to." I crane my neck, looking over Katya's head. That same woman is walking toward us, as if she sensed we were talking about her.

"That's a smart lady," she says, waving the flowers at me before closing her eyes and taking them to her nose.

"You're about to meet her." When I nod, Katya turns around.

"Well, well, look what the cat dragged in for the second day in a row," the old woman says, her face lighting up when she sees me. "Let me guess, this is the girlfriend."

"Yes, this is my girlfriend, Katya." I step back and gesture from the lady to Katya. "Katya, this is woman I teach Russian customs yesterday."

"Real funny," she scowls at me before replacing it with a grin for Katya. She stretches out her wrinkled hand. "You can call me Lucia."

"Lucia. That's a beautiful name." As Katya shakes her hand, the old woman beams.

"Lucia, you own this shop?" I ask as I look around. It's busier in here today than it was yesterday.

"Yup. That's why my name is on the sign."

"Your sign say Vitale."

"Are you sure about this one, Katya? He seems a bit thick." She taps her temple. We both laugh. "Vitale is my last name."

"You liked the tulips so much, you came back for more?" Lucia nods to the flowers Katya's holding. Red tulips—the exact kind she picked out for me yesterday.

"These are my favorite," Katya replies, closing her eyes and bringing the flowers to her nose.

"You know, your boyfriend wasn't sure about the flowers to get you yesterday. I told him to get you red tulips." She sounds proud of her advice.

"Well, thank you," Katya replies. "I bet he told you he needed an odd number, yes?"

"I will admit, he taught me something I didn't know. We don't get many Russians in here." She says conspiratorially.

"Glad I could help," I chime in.

"I'm gonna go save another man from making a stupid flower decision." She laughs. "I hope I see you both again." She seems happy, she must have lived a fulfilled life, a life she truly enjoyed.

"Nice to meet you, Lucia," Katya calls as the woman walks away. When she's out of sight my girlfriend turns to me. "That's it! I'm never leaving Detroit again."

I laugh. "Why is that?"

"That woman has a crush on you!" Katya puts her hand in mine as we stroll to the counter to pay.

13

KATYA

It's been over a month since I've seen Vanya. Between both of our schedules, we haven't had any time to get together. I miss him more than ever, but it'll only be a few more days until I see him. I finally have a free weekend, and I'm flying to New York for the NHL All-Star game where Vanya, and many other Russian players, will be.

Currently, I'm in Los Angeles to shoot a music video for Andres Martinez's latest single. I've been looking forward to this moment ever since Andres' agent told Jill that Andres wanted me to be in the video at the Katya fragrance release party in New York.

I don't think I'd ever been more excited about a project in my life. I've done hundreds of photo shoots—literally hundreds—but this is my first music video. I haven't been able to sleep more than four hours over the last few nights, which has been hard on my body.

The shoot will take two days, but I'll only be needed for a half day on each of them. They're filming the scenes with Andres and his band this morning, and I'm supposed to be on set at around seven p.m. Since becoming a model, I've been around many celebrities and musicians, but I've never met Andres. Which is kind of funny, since we're both based out of Miami. You'd think we would have crossed paths at some point.

After a full day of training and workouts, Jill and I grab a late lunch in L.A. before heading to the studio in Long Beach. I'm whisked straight to hair and make-up. I don't know anything about the concept of the video or what I'll be doing, but since I love being on camera and dancing, I figure I'll be okay.

Once the artists have worked their magic, I'm led to a room with racks of clothes. A stylist hands me a pair of leather, bootcut pants and a black and white top. There's a flurry of activity around me, and I can hear Andres' song piping through the studio. It's catchy, and I find myself already moving my hips as I get dressed.

"You've got nothing to worry about out there, Katya. You've already got the groove," the production assistant tells me as she hands me a jacket.

"It's such a great song," I gush, sliding on the coat.

"Come on." She waves for me to follow her.

Shivering, I tug the jacket closed, as she leads me through the air-conditioned studio to the set. We walk quickly, making sure not to trip over cords and wires as my stiletto heels clack along the floor. A camera crew from a music network follows us, filming the entire process for a behind-the-scenes video.

"Katya!" Andres greets me with a wide, infectious smile.

"Hi, Andres," I say as he grabs my shoulders and kisses me on each cheek. His lips are soft, and he smells like expensive cologne. "It's nice to meet you."

"I'm so happy you agreed to do this. I've been excited to work with you."

"I've been excited as well. I haven't stopped smiling since you asked me.

"That's exactly why I wanted you, Katya! You're always sporting that stunning smile. At that event for your perfume, I told my agent, her!" He points at me. "We need her."

His compliments make my grin even bigger. I feel like my cheeks will explode. With cameras capturing our entire interaction, I make sure to keep my smile and laugh ready. It's not hard, since he's so sweet and makes me feel very comfortable.

I clap my hands together, excited to get started. "I'm ready. Where do you want me? What should I do?"

"You play my love interest in the video."

"Your love interest?" I laugh, hoping it hides my nervousness. I'm actually relieved I didn't know the concept before I got here. How would I have been able to keep that from Vanya? And how would he feel if he knew?

He turns and points behind him where there's a stage and crowd of extras ready to cheer him on. "This is the scene where you're watching me in concert and you get really excited."

"I get excited watching you?" I ask, crossing my arms under my chest. "From the performance, right?"

"Absolutely. The sex scenes are tomorrow."

"Sex scenes?" I ask, rearing back in surprise, but the smile stays on my face. "Is that why you asked me to be on this video?"

"We're totally clothed. Just making out!" He holds his hands up in the air laughing.

"Okay. Okay." I touch his upper arm.

"But this first part, you're in the crowd staring at me, enthralled by my magical voice and how I'm singing just for you."

"Oh, you're singing just for me, yes?" I place both hands over my heart as if swooning. "What are you singing?"

"I will sing anything you want me to." He lifts his arms as if gathering the world for me. "You'll be in the crowd and then everyone will be gone, and it's just us. It's the moment—that passionate moment—when you know you love me." His voice gets higher, more excited, as he talks about the concept.

"Oh wow. Don't get too excited now," I say, laughing and touching his upper arm to bring him down a bit.

"I am excited! I'm standing next to Katya Novikova. Who wouldn't be excited?"

"Oh, whatever." I roll my eyes and wave him off. He's very

charming and complimentary. If I didn't have Vanya in my life, I may be swayed by it.

He points behind him with his thumb and winks. "I gotta get to the stage. Jamie will be over to tell you what you need to do."

I laugh at what a jokester he is. But I appreciate his ability to make me feel very comfortable when I'm a bit nervous.

The sexual nature of the video doesn't intimidate me. Andres Martinez's celebrity persona is all about being a brooding, sensual, Latin-lover. His songs ooze romance and sex, so even without knowing what the video was about, I figured it would be something romantic or sexual. It's not that I'm excited to make out with a random man. I'm excited because it fits with my brand.

The reason I get many of my endorsements and magazine covers is no secret, and it's not because of my stellar tennis skills. I've been sexualized in the American media since my parents and I moved to Florida to work with Charlie when I was fifteen. Articles and news stories have always focused more on my looks than my talent.

I love being in front of the camera. I love being a sex symbol, a fantasy. I love the attention that comes with it. It makes me feel like the strong, beautiful woman I am. Playing up my femininity and sexiness doesn't mean I'm any less of a tennis player. I prove my talent by winning matches—and championships.

Being in a sexy video with an extremely attractive musician doesn't mean I'm going to cheat on my boyfriend. I don't believe in marriage, but I *do* believe in commitment. There aren't any feelings involved. All of my feelings are for Vanya.

Before I take my place in the crowd, the music network asks me a few questions for their footage.

Even though the process is long and intense, I decide quickly that I like acting. The last scene for the night is the last scene of the video, where Andres and I are alone in the crowd. He hooks his fingers into the waistband of my pants and pulls me into his chest. I wrap my arms around him and we embrace until Jamie, the director, yells, "Cut!"

As soon as he yells, we both back away as if the other is on fire. I push my hair back and giggle. "That was so fun. Good job, Andres."

"Ha! Thanks, Katya. You did great. Thank you so much."

"Andres and Katya are done for tonight," Jamie calls out. "We'll see everyone tomorrow. It's going to be a long day, so don't be late."

It's after ten p.m. by the time we finish and the East to West coast time change is taking a toll on me. I'm exhausted and I know it's an early wake-up call to be on set again tomorrow.

When I rest my head on the pillow in my posh LA hotel room, my stomach swirls with excitement. It was an amazing day. Tomorrow, I'll finish the video, then hop on a plane to New York. By nightfall, I'll be in Vanya's arms.

14

VANYA

All Star weekend is always a flurry of activity, only for me, there's much more going on this year than in others. The official NHL events start tonight, but I got into town early because Kirya and I have been discussing a business deal for the past few weeks.

Instead of having the cab take me to my hotel, I give the driver the address to the Russian Dining Room. The bartender directs me to the office downstairs. Over the last couple years, it's undergone a complete renovation. Why anyone would keep the office near the bathrooms is beyond me, but I guess space is limited in New York buildings, and you'd rather have as much patron-space as possible.

As I stand in the doorway, Kirya is behind the desk with his head-down, scribbling something on a paper in front of him. When I knock on the frame, he looks up. Then he stands and approaches me saying,

"Vanya, come in. It's good to see you."

"You too, brother." After we embrace, he returns to his seat and I take the one across from him.

"Did you read the contract?" he asks, reaching onto a shelf and grabbing a bottle of vodka.

I nod as he sets two glasses on the desk. "You didn't add anything since I last looked, did you?"

He looks up from pouring. "Just a twenty percent increase to my agent fee, but nothing else."

"I thought you were supposed to be a silent partner?" I roll my eyes.

"Only on paper, dear brother." He places the paperwork in front of me. "I'm the loudest mother fucker you know."

"If you're going to make all the decisions and tell me what to do, I won't sign."

"Yes, you will, because this gives you a chance to be with Katya more often. New York is her second home, not Detroit," he says, setting the glass next to the contract.

I grab a pen and lean over, my hand hovering over the page. I sign my name quickly, sealing the deal.

With that signature, I became a fifty-percent owner of the Russian Dining Room. The ghost on the other side of the desk owns the other half. But he can't be seen by anyone but me—and whoever else he chooses. One of which is not Stasya.

In order to get my sister out of Russia safely, Kirya faked his death. Well, it wasn't that he faked it as much as he sent her to America with her thinking he was dead—and he ordered everyone to keep it that way.

Stasya doesn't know any different, and it kills me.

She's upstairs right now without a clue that the man she loves is alive and well, right under her feet—literally.

Kirya raises his glass. "To the newest owner of the RDR."

We clink glasses and empty the glasses in one swallow. Then he refills them and we do the same thing. The vodka gives me liquid courage.

"Stasya eats here almost every day. She's going to ask about how the opportunity for me to become an owner came up. She's going to ask who I've partnered with."

"Well then, you'll have to figure out something to tell her, won't you?" Kirya doesn't meet my eyes, keeping busy by filling the glasses again.

"Why are you doing this to her?" I bat the pencil cup off his desk to get some kind of reaction from him. "She's a shell of herself."

He glances at the pens and pencils scattered across the floor, then brings his gaze back to me. Though he looks amused, he's still an intimidating figure—for most. I still think of him as the guy I grew up with—my brother from another woman.

"It looks like she's doing just fine moving on with Morozov." Kirya grabs the papers and rolls his chair to a printer in the corner of the office. He makes a copy of the contract and hands it to me. "She's better off without knowing, without me."

The relationship between Stasya and Dima is laughable. They're like strangers in the same house who may have sex sometimes. I don't know. It's not something I want to think about.

"So, I'm supposed to keep your secret for the rest of my life? And watch my sister wilt?"

"I could have you killed." He shrugs. "Or do it myself."

"You have a sick sense of humor."

"Tell me something I don't know, Vanya." He leans back in his chair and places his left ankle on his right knee, seemingly calm, but I know he's agitated. "Stasya is better off without me," he says firmly.

I push back my chair and stand up before leaning toward him. "You can say it out loud as many times as you want, but you and I both know you'll never believe that."

I knock twice on the desk then walk out.

Sometimes, holding onto Kirya's secret makes me feel like I'm living a double life. I'm down here talking to him, signing paperwork, and then going upstairs to surprise my sister at lunch.

I once joked that Stasya should buy the place, but she already owns it—in a way. She just doesn't know. Everything Kirya owns is split in two names—his and my sister's. If things keep going according to his plan, she won't know until he really is dead.

And I don't say anything because as much as I know Kirya thinks of me as family, I also know what he does to people who cross him.

Stasya's removing her sketchbook from an oversized bag when

she looks up and sees me, her eyes are wide in surprise before a smile spreads across her face.

Normally, the only time we get to see each other are during the summer when I spend time in New York. Every time I see her, the guilt of leaving her behind floods my memories.

Over the years, we've discussed everything that happened at length. She understands I did what I did to protect her. I knew she was in good hands with Kirya, but I also know the pain of betrayal is still there. Since hashing it out, our relationship is almost back to normal. I don't know if she'll ever fully trust me again, but I know she loves me, and she'd never let the grudge stand in the way of our relationship.

I stride toward her, sitting at a tiny two-top at the back of the restaurant. She stands up to greet me. "What are you doing here?"

Instead of answering right away, I pull her toward me and kiss her cheeks. "I am an All-Star, Stasya," I say with exaggeration. "You knew I was coming into town for this weekend."

"Ah, yes." She touches her forehead as if remembering. "Don't you have press conferences and a skills competition to be at?"

"I do. But all of that is later," I say, removing my gray pea coat and throwing it over the chair across from her.

"You act like you own the place," she mumbles, plucking her tea off the table quickly, as if saving it from being spilled.

I laugh. "I do," I tell her. Then, I scan the restaurant, confused as to why she's at this tiny table when she has her pick of the place. "What are we doing at this table? We should be at one of those banquets." I nod to the bright red booth behind her.

"Wait? You what?"

"Let's move," I say, picking up her bag and grabbing both of our coats.

"Well, I didn't expect you—" she stammers as I move everything to one of the huge red booths. She carries her tea to the table and slides in after me.

I lean into the soft cushioning and close my eyes briefly. "Much better."

"Thank you," Stasya says as Sergei, our waiter, sets a steaming bowl of borscht in front of her. It smells amazing and reminds me of how hungry I am.

She places her napkin across her lap and picks up her spoon before lifting her eyes to me. "Please tell me what's going on."

"You are looking at the Russian Dining Room's newest owner. I just signed the papers."

"You bought this place?" she asks.

"I bought into it." I raise my hand to grab Sergei's attention before he walks away. "This is my retirement, Stasya."

The waiter is back at our table in two point five seconds. "Mr. Kravtsov, welcome. What can I get you?"

"A bottle of Stolichnaya. We're celebrating."

Sergei nods. "Very good, Sir."

"Work is not a wolf, Vanya. It doesn't run to the woods."

Hearing my sister use a Russian saying brings warmth to my heart. It's a familiarity that I rarely feel here in America. They have their own proverbs and idioms that I don't always quite understand. It's a reminder that home isn't necessarily a place, it's who you're with. I think about Katya and how being with her feels like home.

"Not today, Stasya. You will take this day off and celebrate with your brother."

It's just after noon on a cold Friday in January. I know she has workers who can take care of her store when she's not there.

"You really think you should be drinking when you have the skills event tonight?"

"That's nothing. It's all fun." I assure her. "Do you think I forget how to skate and shoot after a few drinks?"

"I don't think you'll forget; I worry your aim will be off. Someone might lose an eye."

"Would you like me to aim for Dima's head?" I ask. "Or lower?"

Dima and I have been friends for years. In some ways, we're more like brothers are than just former teammates.

"Don't give him any reason to be even more temperamental. He has enough mood swings during the season."

"Dima has always been intense."

Sergei returns to the table with the Stoli and two glasses. I wait as the waiter pours the vodka for us before setting the bottle down.

"He will be in a good mood tomorrow. I promise you this. I've invited everyone back here after the game to celebrate before we all go on our way again."

"Everyone?" she asks, lifting her eyes from her spoonful of soup.

"Not everyone," I clarify, picking up both glasses and holding one out to her. "Just the Russians."

"Where do the Americans and Canadiens go?"

"Fuck if I know," I say, slamming my drink. My stomach is already warm from the shots I had while signing the contract earlier. I push the glass toward my sister. "Come on, Stasya."

She shakes her head. "I told you I have too much work to do today."

"You're so serious all the time. One of these days, you will let loose and enjoy yourself again."

When I see tears in her eyes, I realize my comment may have been a little insensitive. Despite her brave, stoic demeanor, she's still wrecked over Kirya. It takes everything I have not to tell her what I know, but I can't. It was in the contract.

"Let me know when that day will be, Vanya. I'll look forward to it." A tear slides down, but she wipes it away quickly.

I inch closer, slide my arm across her shoulders and pull her into my side. When she drops her cheek onto my shoulder, I kiss the top of her head. "You will get through this, Stasya. You are strong and resilient."

She lets me hold her for a beat, before inhaling deeply and saying, "Pass me that drink."

15

KATYA

I arrive in New York just in time for the Saturday night All-Star weekend celebration. After the game that afternoon, the Russian players who came into town descend on the Russian Dining Room, hungry for a delicious dinner. Though many of them played against each other, there's nothing but happiness and comradery among them.

Vanya and my ex-boyfriend, Zhenya, both played for the winning team, the Western Conference. I thought hanging around my ex when Vanya and I are obviously together would be awkward, but it isn't. With all the career pressure and media covering my every move, drama with a former flame is the last thing I need.

Exhaustion hits me like a brick, but I'm always ready for a party. And this is one of the best ones I've been to in years. All Russians, an amazing meal of familiar favorites, and being with the man I love.

After the cab drops me off, I dash through the doors of the iconic Russian restaurant, bubbling with excitement. Everyone else has been there for at least an hour. The noise level gets louder and louder as the waiter leads me to a separate room called the Bear Salon. It's a good thing they put our group away from the main dining room because the more this crowd drinks, the louder it will get.

When I enter, I spot Vanya standing at the bar with his sister, Stasya, and her boyfriend, Dima. He's smiling brightly with his arms extended as if telling some story. I run to him and rush into those open arms.

"There you are," he says, wrapping his arms around me and holding me tightly. "I've missed you, Sunshine."

"I've missed you more!" I rise onto my toes and offer my lips.

Vanya doesn't disappoint, kissing me like we're the only two people in the room right there in front of his sister. He slides his hands over my back and down to my leather-clad butt. I loved the pants from the video shoot so much, I bought them. Not only did *I* love them, but I knew Vanya would love me in them. I've paired it with a sheer black tank top with spaghetti straps. He hasn't seen that yet because I still have a sexy motorcycle jacket on.

"Don't eat her face off," Dima quips.

We pull back and gaze into each other's eyes for a moment before coming back to reality.

"Your ass feels amazing," Vanya whispers to me, squeezing my cheeks. I step back, put my hands on my hips, and twirl as if I'm in a commercial modeling the pants. Then I pop my hip so he has a perfect view.

"Do you like them?" I ask.

"It's good to see you again, Katya," Stasya interrupts.

I turn around quickly and give her a hug, kissing her cheeks three times. "Stasya! Please excuse my manners. I haven't seen your brother in over a month. I missed him terribly."

"I understand." She touches my arm and leans closer. "Your ass looks amazing. I wish I had those pants at *Prekrasny*. Maybe I need to make a pair."

"If you make them, I'd buy them."

Vanya puts his hand on my back. "Come on, ladies. Let's sit and catch up. I'm dying to hear about the music video."

I bite my lip, but follow Stasya to the table. I didn't do anything wrong, yet the sweat beading on my forehead makes me feel like I'm guilty of something. My heart races as I take off my jacket and hang it on the back of a chair before sliding into a huge red booth.

I scoot closer to Vanya, so close he has to put his arm around me to sit comfortably. But that's exactly what I want. I've missed him so much over the last month. All I can think of is molding myself into his body and having him inside me.

"How was it? Tell me everything," he says.

After two hours, we've talked and laughed and gone through I-don't-know-how-many bottles of vodka. Every time we set our glasses down, someone is making another toast, as is Russian custom.

This time, it's Zhenya standing up, raising his glass, and addressing the entire table. "To Pavel Viktorovich Myshkin! For without him, none of us would be here!"

His toast is met with a mixed reaction: a chorus of groans with a few laughs peppered in. Myshkin was the revered head coach of the CSA when most of these guys left. From what Vanya told me, many players respected him as their coach but disliked him as a person. Instead of earning his position, he was appointed to it, and many didn't think he deserved it. He had a strict coaching style and demanded full control over his player's lives. It was so bad, a few guys, like Vanya, chose defection over playing for him anymore. Myshkin feared his best men would defect so much that he cut the ones—like Dima Morozov—who had been drafted by the NHL from the team.

Still, Zhenya is right. Without him as their coach, some of these guys might have stayed with the system rather than make the leap to a better life in North America.

After the toast, Vanya wiggles out from my grasp and stands up.

His sister, Stasya, props her elbows on the table and drops her head into her hands. "I can't take another drink," she pleads with him.

"You can sit this one out, Stasya." Vanya winks at her. Then, he raises his glass and continues, "Times like this remind me that home isn't necessarily a place, it's who you're with. To friendship!"

"To friendship!" The chorus repeats and we all drink.

When Vanya sits, I place my hand on his thigh and lean into kiss him. My head is fuzzy, my stomach is full, I've never been so content.

Dima returns to the table with a silly grin on his lips. Stasya scoots out of the booth to let him in, wavering a bit as she does. He grabs her waist, pulls her into his arms, and plants his lips on her. She falls into him, clutching his shoulders as they kiss.

It's quite passionate and romantic. I bump Vanya's shoulder with mine and nod in the direction of his sister and her boyfriend.

Stasya's mouth forms the word, "Wow."

They've pulled apart, but stay clutched in an embrace, speaking quietly to each other. I look away, thinking it's not right to watch such an intimate moment.

Suddenly, Dima sweeps a glass of champagne from the table and drops to one knee. I slap Vanya's thigh three times quickly, to get his attention.

"What is it, love?" he asks.

"He's doing it," I whisper with excitement. We both know what's coming. Dima talked to Vanya about it a few weeks ago.

Stasya bends over, looking concerned like he may be hurt. "Dima! Are you—"

He lifts his head, looking into her eyes as he raises the flute.

"I'm sorry, I can't drink any more tonight," she says.

He whispers something to her but I can't tell what he says despite complete silence at the table. Everyone is rapt with their attention on Dima and Stasya.

She appears confused as she peers into the glass. She seems to notice something because her eyes are wide as she brings her hands up to cover her mouth with her hands. There's a bit of chatter as people realize what's happening, but the volume in the room is considerably lower.

Stasya glances over her shoulder at Vanya. With one raised eyebrow and a smirk, his face holds no trace of surprise.

"Anastasiya," Dima begins, using her full name.

When her gaze shifts back to Dima, Stasya's face is pink, and her chest rises and falls quickly. She looks frightened rather than excited.

"Will you marry me?" he asks with shaking hands.

Though I'm not the one being proposed to, my stomach swirls, and my heart races, excited to be here for such a beautiful moment. Under the table, Vanya squeezes my hand.

Instead of answering, Stasya stands frozen, looking at Dima with an expression of mixed emotions.

We're all waiting with bated breath on her answer. The silence starts to get uncomfortable.

I lean close to Vanya's ear and whisper, "What's going on?"

He shrugs and shakes his head, but doesn't take his gaze off his sister.

Suddenly, Dmitri's smile falters, and he squeaks out, "Stasya?"

"Um, sure," she says, nodding, as if remembering she's supposed to say something.

Though the table erupts into cheers as Dmitri slams the champagne and fishes a ring from the bottom of the flute. He grabs Stasya's hand and slides it onto her finger. Then he stands up and pulls her into his arms.

"To Dima and Stasya!"

"To a beautiful life together!"

"Let the tables break from abundance, and the beds break from love!"

Despite the excitement from everyone else, I can't help but feel like Stasya isn't happy about the proposal. I'm not sure if it's because she felt awkward being put on the spot or because Dima did something so personal in front of all these people, but her smile seems forced and it doesn't reach her eyes. Her gaze darts around the room as if she needs to get away.

It's no surprise when she excuses herself to use the restroom.

"Is Stasya okay?" I ask Vanya, watching with worry as she hurries toward the front of the restaurant. "Should I go with her?"

He shakes his head. "I knew it wouldn't be easy for her. Give her a minute."

"What do you mean? I thought she and Dima were quite happy together."

His brows furrow as he watches his sister rush to the front of the restaurant. “Stasya has been through a lot. I think her feelings are complicated.”

“Do you want to go with her?” I ask, understanding if he wants to check on her.

He shakes his head. “I’ll give her a minute to process.”

16

VANYA

After practice, Mike Collins, Ricky Campbell, Petr Novotný, and I head to Hoover's, a small restaurant not far from the Chargers arena. The bartender nods hello and tells us he'll be over with menus in a minute.

"We're heading to the VIP section," Campbell calls. He nods to the table in the back of the restaurant that we sit at every time we're here.

"Nothing but the best for my boys," Flo, the only waitress who's ever working in this place, says as she sets a menu in front of each of us.

Novotný picks his up. "Do we even need these?"

"Cheeseburgers and fries all around." She jots the order on her notepad.

"And—" Campbell starts.

"I know! I know!" She waves at him with her pen. "No lettuce for that one and give your pickle to the Russian." She looks at us over her thick black glasses. "I'll be back with a bucket of beers."

"You're the perfect woman, Flo. You always know exactly what men want."

"Save it for the puck bunnies, Romeo."

"You just got shot down by a seventy-year-old woman," Collins teases.

Hoovers isn't crowded at all, which is normal for the dinner hour. Things kick up after nine. And when I say that, I mean ten to fifteen people tops.

"I think I'm okay with that." Campbell shoots Collins the middle finger. He seems to notice something out of the corner of his eye and turns his head. "Maybe I'll have better luck with those two stone-cold foxes."

Two women glance at us, then look away as if playing coy. But we all know, they aren't shy. They're puck bunnies, the girls who actively seek out hockey players. I have no problem with bunnies. They aren't my cup of tea, but they make it easy for guys on nights they don't feel like searching for someone.

I chuckle and lean back in my chair, making room as Flo reaches over me to set down a bucket of beers.

"Come on over, ladies." Campbell waves them to the table. They don't have to be asked twice, practically falling over each other to get to us. Instead of standing at the table to interact, they pull up chairs.

"Oh wow," Novotný says, scooting over to make room.

"What's your name, gorgeous?" The blonde sitting next to Campbell asks, smiling and touching his cheek.

He pulls back. "You don't know who I am?"

I put my hand over my mouth to stifle a laugh. Not only is it hilarious because he thinks he's wanted by anything in a skirt, but also because the boys and I always love seeing him to get knocked down when he says things that make him sound like an egomaniac.

She points to me. "That's Ivan Kravtsov over there, but your face isn't familiar."

"Damn, that's cold." Collins laughs, holding his bottle out. Both Novotný and I clink the neck with ours.

"He is goalie," I say. "He have no face."

"Oh, Vanya." The one next to me smiles and places her hand on my arm.

I look from her hand to her face without a smile. "It's Ivan."

She removes her hand, but she's not deterred. She leans closer to me, asking, "So tell us, boys. What are some things you like?"

"Beer." Collins drains his bottle, then slams it down, and grabs another.

"Hockey," Novotný deadpans.

"Sexy women," Campbell winks.

"I like my girlfriend and not being bothered while I eat." I pick up my beer and take a long drink, hoping I've turned her off for good.

The last few months have been the best of my life. Katya and I have spent as much time as we possibly can together, getting closer and having so much fun. A relationship I thought would be stressful and hard to maintain has been fairly seamless. And when we're not together, I have great teammates to hang out with.

"Look who's on the news," Collins cuts in before the girls can ask any more questions. His eyes are focused on something over my head.

"Who?" the blond asks.

Collins points to the television in the corner. I glance quickly, but when I see the logo of a music television network in the corner, I spin back and take a sip of my beer. "Madonna have new boyfriend?"

"Oh shit," Collins hisses.

"Not Madonna." Campbell shakes his head slowly.

"Hey!" Novotný pats my shoulder. "I'm going to grab us another round. Join me?"

"We have beer." I give him a confused look.

Collins and Campbell eyes are still glued to the screen, while Novotný glances at it uncomfortably.

When I look at the T.V. again, my eyes widen with shock, and my jaw drops. I blink rapidly, thinking my sight might be playing tricks on me, but it isn't. What I'm seeing is real.

It's Katya kissing Andres Martinez, the singer who asked her to be in his video earlier this year. There's no sound, but it's not needed. First, it's them kissing on a street. Then they're lying in the backseat of a car. He's covering her body with his, sliding his hands up and down her body and kissing her neck.

"What the fuck?" I jump up, but the clip ends, and the show moves on to something else. "What is this?" I ask out loud. It's not directed at my teammates, but they answer anyway.

"It's probably just—" Collins begins, but he can't finish the thought because no one has an explanation.

"Oh my god! She's so lucky. Andres is sex on a stick."

"This is man she have video with," I tell them, dropping into my chair.

Three of the five heads whip around to look at me. The girls are still looking at the T.V.

"What?" I ask confused.

Collins drops his beer onto the table, but quickly grabs it before it falls. "Like, a sex tape?"

"No." I shake my head in disgust. "She in his music video."

"Ohhhh," they all chorus.

"How is this news?" the blonde asks. "Katya and Andres have been in every tabloid and celebrity magazine on the shelves. They're so cute together."

"How she do this? Why she do this?" I rest my elbows on the table and let my head fall into my hands.

"Hey, hey, take it easy," Collins says. "She's always all over the news, right? The press takes pictures and makes things out to be worse than they are."

"She's getting fucked in the back of a car," Campbell says dryly. Novotný punches his shoulder. "What?"

"They're fully clothed."

"Sorry!" He holds his hands up. "They're dry humping in the back of a car. If my girl ever did that. I'd never forgive her."

"Probably why you don't have a girl."

I slide my chair back from the table and stand up abruptly. Then I dig into my pocket, take money out of my wallet, and throw it on the table.

"Come on, V! You don't need to get into it tonight," Novotný calls. "Sleep on it."

"I sleep for months," I say, storming to the exit and leaving my friends behind. I'm stewing as I walk to my car.

I know the paparazzi love Katya and follow her around. I know they take pictures and create stories to sell copies. I never thought I had to worry because I've always trusted, Katya. She never gave me a reason not to.

Now, I'm beginning to wonder what happened in Los Angeles while she was making that video. She told me her part was acting as the singer's love interest. A love interest is the pretty girl in the video who the singer lusts for. She's smiling and dancing, not kissing and simulating sex.

When I get in the car, I slam the steering wheel with the palm of my hand. How could I be so stupid to think she was ready to settle down with one man? Especially at her age and with her popularity. She's the *it* girl that everyone wants.

This is exactly the kind of distraction I didn't want. As if the stress of trying to find time to see each other with two busy schedules wasn't enough, the jealousy of seeing her all over the place with other people was bound to take a toll.

Instead of calming down on the ride home, I'm actually more worked up. I run to the phone in the kitchen and dial her number.

After five rings, she finally picks up. "Hello?" Her voice sounds as if she's been sleeping.

"Katya,"

"Vanya, love." I can hear her smile through the phone. "What's going on? You're calling late."

"You're all over the news!" I yell.

"All over the news? What are you talking about?' She asks through a yawn.

"Photos of you and the singer," I snap, slamming my palm on my kitchen counter.

"Oh Vanya, it's probably just photos from the video. You know what the press says about me."

I hear the squeak of a bed frame as if she sat up or jumped out of bed.

"You were kissing him, Katya. Kissing him and laying with him." My voice breaks towards the end, but my anger is intact. "He was all over you."

"I told you I was his love interest in the video. It was just acting, Vanya." Her voice is nonchalant, as if I should understand.

"Acting? Having sex with someone is acting, now? You weren't in a film, Katya. It was a music video. You could have said no. You could have drawn the line."

"We didn't have sex!" She yells back. "This is absolutely ridiculous."

"Yes, it is ridiculous that you had no problem doing that when you have a boyfriend."

"This is my life, Vanya. I'm a model and a sex symbol. You knew that from the first moment we started this."

"You're right, I did know that. But I thought you had integrity."

"Excuse me?"

"That's not what I meant. I—" I backtrack, scrambling for words to apologize but Katya cuts me off.

"You know what, Vanya? This relationship isn't working for me anymore." Her voice is ice and getting colder with every word. "I need someone who understands my life and trusts me." It's the last thing she says before slamming down the receiver.

My brain is numb as I hang up the phone. She broke up with me. I don't know what my intention was when I called, but that certainly wasn't it. Things had been going great between us for months and in less than five minutes, everything blew up.

Maybe we didn't have the foundation I thought we did.

17

VANYA

The last month and a half has been a rollercoaster of emotions, I don't have words to describe it—in English or Russian. During the season, I tallied seventy-seven goals, a personal and team record. And the Chargers have had the ride of our lives: capturing the President's trophy as the team with the most points in the league and winning all three of the playoff series we've played so far.

And I've done it all without Katya by my side.

Hence the rollercoaster. How can I enjoy the ride when I haven't been able to celebrate the best season of my hockey career with the person I love the most?

We haven't talked since I saw the tabloid photos of her and Andres. I could barely handle the risqué music video—but to see the photos of them together in a Hollywood nightclub was too much. That didn't fall under the category of "work." That was all play.

We cruised through the playoffs, scaling every hurdle, and defeating every team we came across on our way to the Stanley Cup Finals. A best-selling author couldn't have written a better story.

And now, here we are, in the intermission before the third period of Game 7 against the New York Americans on their home ice. I've been matched up against Dima Morozov, one of my best friends, for the entire series, and I don't expect that to change.

Years ago, I made the conscious choice to defect from the USSR for the opportunity to play in the National Hockey League with the best players in the world. I abandoned the only country I knew and my entire family for the chance at this moment.

My sister is in the stands. And even though she's here because Dima plays for the Americans, I know deep down she's cheering for me. Our bond is too strong for it to go any other way.

The person of significance that's missing is Katya. And the weight of her absence hits on me hard.

But not hard enough to take me out of the zone.

I made a commitment to the Chargers when I made the decision to defect.

This moment has been the dream of every single man in this room for as long as they can remember. As I glance around the locker room, some of the guys are silent, with their heads down. A few have their eyes are closed, others have knees shaking with nervous energy. And though the Cup has been my dream for a slightly shorter time, I feel the pressure.

Just then, Coach Gagnon walks in and the room falls silent. He looks around, his eyes settling on every face present before he clears his throat and asks, "Are you fucking ready?"

"Yes sir!" The entire team yells together.

"I said, are you fucking ready?" he asks again, louder this time, the muscles on his neck straining to show the extra effort.

"YES SIR!" We chorus together again. It's much louder than the first time, and some guys bang against the lockers to make extra noise.

We know exactly how to respond, since this has been our pre-game ritual ever since we won that first playoff game in April.

Hockey players are superstitious.

"Let's pump it up. We are here in Game Seven of the Stanley Cup

Finals for a fucking reason. We're a fucking good hockey team." His cheeks are red, and he's pointing with his index finger to punctuate every sentence. "And we're going to fucking bring the Cup home to Detroit tonight. So, let's fucking go!"

Every guy in the room jumps up, inspired by Coach's short, enthusiastic speech. There's a chorus of:

"Let's go boys!"

"Let's do this!"

I adjust my shoulder pads and grab my helmet and stick. As I follow my teammates to the ice, my mind is far away. Coach's words echo through my head. We're in Game 7 for a reason. I know he means our hard work and determination in every game this season got us to where we are, and we deserve it.

I'm thinking about the reason *I'm* here, the reason *I* play. It's been years since I really thought about it. While it's true, I play for myself, for the freedom—and opportunities—hockey's allowed me to have.

But above all, I play for my team. The unit who has a common goal and does everything together—win or lose. I may be living in America, but I'm still a Soviet man. I can't forget my upbringing: being selfless, sacrificing everything for the cause. Playing a professional sport, being part of a team, isn't about me, it's about *us*.

* * *

OVER THE LAST five minutes of the third period, my teammates and I have thrown everything we have at the Americans, trying to score to break the 3-3 deadlock.

The announcer says something over the PA that causes the crowd to respond with a thunderous cheer. Using the praise as motivation, I jump off the bench and join the play, accepting a pass from Collins on defense and skating up the ice. When I pass the blue line, I see a shot and take it, rearing my stick back and slamming it against the puck. The American's goalie reaches out quickly, grabbing it with his glove and holding on until the ref blows the whistle.

I remove my mouth guard and look up at the scoreboard, hocking spit onto the ice before I return the guard back to its place. There's thirty seconds on the clock, and the game is tied 3-3. My stomach is in my throat, but this is where I excel—now-or-never situations.

The ref drops the puck. I win the faceoff, sending it back to Collins in one swift motion, but he's immediately checked and loses control. New York takes the puck and turns it around, charging toward Campbell, our goalie.

American's rookie forward, Tremblay, rears back before sending the puck forward with everything he has.

Skating forward, evading bodies as I close in on the goal, ready to pick up a rebound, I watch the puck fly. For a moment everything is silent. All yelling from the players on the ice is blocked out. The sharp sound as skates glide over the ice is blocked out. The noise from the crowd is blocked out. In that moment, all I can hear is my heavy breathing, as my eyes follow the puck.

It sails right through Ricky's five hole. The red light goes off and the crowd erupts. The noise from the fans is deafening, in all my years, I've never heard anything like it.

As the Americans celebrate, my teammates and I skate to the bench to get the play from Coach Gagnon.

Adrenaline pumps through my veins, refusing to give up. There's still 1.6 seconds left. It's a long shot, but we have to try.

Everyone in the arena is on their feet, buzzing with anxiety and excitement. I'm shifting my weight from foot to foot, willing myself to use that momentum to spur me on.

Skating into the circle to face me is Dan McDonald, the veteran center who never wears a helmet. I'm not nervous to face him. I'm nervous because this is the most important faceoff of my life.

The puck drops.

Dan wins the draw, sending it to a defenseman behind him.

The clock strikes zero.

And the entire arena erupts, everyone jumping to their feet screaming and cheering. On the ice, the Americans throw their gloves and sticks before crashing the net.

I bend at the waist and rest my stick on my thighs in disbelief. Then, it's as if I can't hold my weight anymore. I drop to my knees and look up at the scoreboard one last time before hanging my head again.

When I finally have the energy, I skate over to the bench to join the rest of my team watching the Americans celebrate. There's nothing worse than having to watch the other team celebrate after you just lost the most important game of your life. But we have to hang around for the center ice handshake.

Actually, I'm wrong—that handshake is worse than having to watch the other team celebrate. Don't get me wrong, I think it's a great tradition. At the end of the day, we're all out there doing our jobs and playing the game we love. To show each other respect after a hard-fought series is something I appreciate.

But it fucking sucks when you lose.

When we finally get back to the locker room, it's silent, except for the sound of gear slamming into lockers and skates shuffling across the floor. Thankfully, we have a few minutes to compose ourselves before the media will be allowed in. The press is the last thing I want to deal with tonight. The media. The flashing cameras. Pretending to be calm and poised on such a disappointing night.

I already know what they'll say about me. It's the same thing they've said every year since I joined the Chargers. I don't have the heart. Russians don't show up because we don't care about the Stanley Cup. That I "only" had six goals in this series, why didn't I do more?

I take a deep breath, wishing I didn't know enough English to answer. Wishing Vitya were next to me.

Thankfully, the press doesn't stay long, finally having a little mercy on us and letting us wallow in peace. Like most of my teammates, I can't get out of the locker room fast enough. We can still hear the celebration vibrating through the arena. After showering and collecting my things, I push the door open and slide out quietly. When I look up, Stasya stands in the hallway, biting her thumbnail.

She rushes to me and throws her arms around me. I slump in her embrace, my stoic facade falling for a moment. When I notice water dripping from the tips of my wet, shaggy hair onto her shoulder, I pull back.

Tears well in my eyes, but they'll never fall in public, not even in front of my sister.

"Thank you," I say, voice shaking with emotion.

"Of course."

"What are you doing here?" I ask, standing straight and regaining my composure. "You should be with Dima."

"They're still—" she stops. We both know they're still on the ice celebrating because we can still hear the roar of the crowd.

"Dima is the first Russian to win a Stanley Cup. The Dining Room will be hopping tonight." I smile.

"Are you staying or is the team flying out tonight?" she asks, ignoring my question.

I lean against the wall. "Some of the guys are leaving, but most are staying. A lot of them have family here who don't have flights out until tomorrow."

"What are *you* doing?" She reaches out to fix the collar of my suit coat. That simple act sends a flood of emotion through me, and I swallow hard. Knowing someone loves me and cares about me is what I needed.

"Can I stay at your apartment?"

Above the store my sister owns, there's a beautiful apartment she fixed up to be used by visitors. As far as I know, my grandmother and I are the only people who have ever stayed there.

"Of course," she assures me, rubbing my back. "Is Katya in town?"

I look up to the ceiling. "We broke up."

"I'm sorry, Vanya. I didn't know."

She tries to grab my hand, but I wave her away. "It's no problem, seriously."

"Do you want company?"

What in the world is she talking about? Her fiancé just won the Stanley Cup. That comes before wallowing with me—the brother who left her stranded in the USSR while he defected to a better life.

"You think Dima will let you hang out with me tonight?"

"What is this 'let me?' Like I'm some kind of kept woman." She scowls. Any other day, I'd laugh, but I can't find it in my heart right now.

"It's a big night for him, Stasya."

"And it's a difficult night for you. He'll be celebrating all night. He won't even know I'm not there. Who needs me more?

"He will be your husband soon."

"No." She shakes her head. "I don't think he will."

I raise one eyebrow, hoping she continues. Does she know Kirya is alive?

"We can talk at the apartment."

* * *

BEFORE I MET KATYA, every time I was in New York, I stayed at my sister's apartment above her store. That's where we head tonight. When we get there, Stasya goes right to the kitchen and makes us both a cup of tea. I shrug off my coat and kick off my shoes before collapsing on the couch.

She hands me a mug and sits next to me, curling one leg under her.

"How long have you known, Vanya?" she asks quietly, not meeting my eyes.

Her question takes me off guard. I thought she'd ask about Katya or want to console me over the loss. "Known what?"

"How long have you known that Kirya was alive?" She's biting her bottom lip when she looks up at me, as if she's holding back.

"A while," I say.

"Just tell me the truth, Vanya!" When she raises her voice, her entire body shakes and tea spills onto her lap. Tears seep out of the corners of her eyes. "I can't take any more secrets and lies."

My stomach drops. How many times can I break my sister's heart? I reach out, take the cup, and place it on the coffee table. "I've always known."

She doesn't look surprised as she wipes at the tears. "It's what I get for getting involved with the mafia, right?"

"You can't help who you fall in love with."

She laughs, but there's no humor. "I found out the night Dima proposed to me."

My eyes widen. That doesn't make any sense. "I was there that night. You—you said yes to Dima."

"It was after," she whispers. "When I went to the bathroom."

I don't know what to say. With as vigilant as Kirya has been about not wanting Stasya to know about him for three years, it doesn't make sense that he'd slip up.

"How?" I shake my head. "Did he come to you?"

"No. He was walking in just as I was coming back up the stairs. It rattled him." She wipes her nose. "But not as rattled as I was. I've been seeing him ever since, Vanya. I can't help myself. I can't stop. Kirya is my past, my present, *and* my future. He's my soul. I can't live without my soul."

It's as if she's confessing sins to me.

"I'm not here to judge you, Stasya. But if Kirya is your future, you need to tell Dima."

She nods, swallowing hard and rubbing her eyes.

After two hours of talking with my sister, I'm exhausted. I finally convince her to go celebrate with Dmitri, even if it's only for a little while.

"Stasya, I'm fine," I say. "I don't know what you two are going through right now, but I know you. I know your heart better than anyone on this earth. And you're not such a mean person that you would leave him on such an important night for his career. You should be there to celebrate with him."

She nods and gets up quickly.

I grab her hands. "I'm not kicking you out of your own apartment."

"I know, Vanya. You're right. I should be there with him." She reaches out and touches my cheek. "Thank you."

Without another word, she grabs her purse and leaves.

I lock the door behind her, then shuffle to the bedroom, wondering why love has to be so complicated.

18

KATYA

My heart breaks for Vanya. He's had the best year of his life. I've seen how focused he's been on his game and his team. He put blood, sweat, and tears into being a leader and helping take his team to the series hockey players dream their entire lives about—the Stanley Cup Finals.

And they lost.

I've been at every game, traveling from New York to Detroit as if I were a player on either team. As soon as the buzzer sounded to end the game, I ran to the visitor's locker room to wait for him. I may be the last person he wants to see right now when he's already at his lowest, but I need him to see me. I need him to know I'll be with him through the good and the bad. I need him know how I feel.

Then I saw his sister, pacing the hallway outside the locker room, chewing her nails, and I realize how selfish it is to show up like this. It's not my place to be here, to try to console him when we haven't spoken in over a month. Before anyone sees me, I spin around and rush toward the exit to hail a cab back to my hotel.

When I set my key on the dresser, I catch a glimpse of myself in the mirror, all dressed up as if I'm going to a party. And all I feel is shame. When I got ready for the night, I was prepared to meet with

Vanya during a celebration. Prepared to pop into his life at his happiest moment, where he'd be so excited to see me, we wouldn't need to have any discussion about getting back together.

Angerly, I tug the silver hoop earrings out and kick off my Louboutin heels, removing the rest of my clothes as I head to the bathroom. If I do this, I'm going to do it right.

THE CAB DROPS me off in front of *Prekrasny*, the clothing store Vanya's sister owns on W. 57th Street. It's been closed for hours, which is fine, because it's not the store I'm here for. It's the person in the apartment above it.

I race up the stairs, taking two at a time, which is easy in my tennis shoes. Before I knock, I take a deep breath and reach up to tighten my ponytail. I rap on the door while letting out the breath.

After a few seconds, I check my watch, then look behind me. The stairwell only goes to this door, so I'm not sure what I'm looking for. I knock again, harder this time.

Behind the door, I hear shuffling, then the sound of the lock.

"Katya?" Vanya asks, disoriented as he blinks. "What are you doing here?"

His sleepy eyes widen, and he runs his hand through his hair, looking behind me as if I've brought others. There's a towel wrapped around his waist, but his hair isn't wet.

"I—" I pause, gathering strength to look him in the eye. "I had to see you. Especially after—" I cover my face with one hand, losing my nerve now that I'm in front of him. "I'll always be here for you, Vanya. Through good and bad." I turn around and move toward the steps.

"Katya! Wait!"

I spin toward him, but can't meet his eyes.

"Come in." He moves aside, giving me space to enter. I nod and slide past him, my elbow grazing his bare torso. A shiver courses through me.

As the door closes, I feel a tug at my hair. When I spin around Vanya has a small smile on his lips.

"It's straight," he says, absently. I tilt my head, but before I can ask, he continues. "It's usually got some waves and tangles when it's up like that." He wiggles his fingers as he speaks. "You wear it straight when you go out."

Tears prick at my eyes. "I was at the game. I've been at every game of this series."

He looks toward the kitchen and chuckles. "It's two a.m. Did you join the Russians celebrating at the Dining Room?"

"No, I went to my hotel afterwards." I clasp my hands together and twist my fingers. "I came here to tell you that I'm sorry."

"There's always next year, right?" he says, lowering his head.

"No, not the game." I close my eyes and shake my head. "Well, yes, I'm sorry about the game—the series, but I mean I'm sorry about the video and the photos and—" The words come out quickly, saying them all in almost one breath.

"Katya, don't," he says. "I'm the one who owes you an apology. I let the stress get to me. It made me insecure and jealous and I said things I regret."

I grab his hands and plead, "Let's not do this, Vanya. If we rehash everything it won't make any difference. It won't solve anything."

He nods. "I know."

"I love you." I bring his hands to my lips and kiss his fingers as I lift my gaze to his. "I can't stop thinking about you."

He holds my gaze. "I love you, too. I'm sorry I didn't say anything when you told me you loved me. I froze, froze like the coward that I am."

"You're not a coward," I whisper. "I never thought that."

"You mean everything to me, Katya. You are the sunshine that brightens my day and the darkness that lets me rest. Your strength enhances my own. My heart is completely open to you. I love you, Katya," he says.

If he keeps talking, I'll start crying, and all I want is to have his arms around me.

"Forget this talk. I need you." I grab his face and pull it to mine, kissing him with a vibrant passion. He presses back, his tongue finding its way inside my mouth, massaging mine until we're clashing. As we kiss, his deft fingers unzip my warm up jacket and shove it off my shoulders with urgency. The towel at his waist drops onto my shoes. His erection on display.

He pulls away, grabbing the hem of my tank top, dragging it up my body and over my head. I'm breathless when he tugs my hand and leads me to the bedroom, leaving a trail of clothing in our wake.

I need him like a fish needs water—to live. We kiss like tomorrow will never come, hands in each other's hair, going at it with unparalleled intensity, the manifestation of our pent-up desires. By the time he backs me onto the bed, we're both naked, and I'm pulsing with need.

I fall onto my back, Vanya climbs over me, leans down, and presses his lips on mine. I reach up and grab his waist, pulling his pelvis toward me. When his cock hits my entrance, I inhale deeply, and when he thrusts into me, I cry out.

"Oh Vanya, oh!" I moan into this mouth, letting my eyelids flutter shut.

"Don't close your eyes," he orders, thrusting into me with every command. "Look at me. Feel me."

I do as I'm told, opening my eyes and using all of my senses to experience him. I grab onto him, digging my nails into his back and biting his shoulder, letting my tongue taste the salt on his skin. He rolls his pelvis into me, creating delicious friction on my clit as he fills me completely.

He looks into my eyes, a mix of softness and desire. "I love you, Katya."

"I love you," I say as I hit my peak.

EPILOGUE
VANYA

I can't remember falling asleep, but when I wake up, Katya is in my arms, sleeping peacefully with her head on my chest. I run my hand over her back gently, thinking about how amazing it feels to have her here.

Somehow, the worst day of my career turned into the best day of my personal life.

The yin and yang of life.

I kiss her forehead and wiggle out of bed slowly, so I don't wake her. After using the bathroom and taking a quick shower, I shuffle to the kitchen to make coffee.

After a double-take, I realize Katya is sitting on the couch, completely naked with her legs spread.

I rub the back of my neck. "What? How? I thought you were still in bed."

"I was hungry," she says, watching me as she slides a hand across her stomach and down to her pussy. "Aren't you hungry, Vanya?"

That's all the invitation I need.

I rush to the couch, and kneel before her, grabbing her hips and replacing her hand with my mouth. When I plunge my tongue inside her, she bucks off the couch, but I don't let up.

Instead, hook one arm around her thigh and place a hand on her stomach, licking and lapping. She cries out, grabs my hair, and circles her hips. I lift my eyes to watch her as I make her squirm and moan.

"Vanya!" She screams out, then her voice is soft. "Oh, oh, oh."

Her pleasure has me harder than a steel rod. I remove my mouth, slap her outer thigh, and stand up. "Turn around and get on your knees."

Without another word, she flips over, gets on her knees, and clutches the back of the couch, while I guide my cock to her pussy, sliding into her slowly.

"Yes, Katya! Oh my god!" I squeeze her hips, excited by the sight of her tight, toned ass as I slide in and out of her. I trail my hand down her back, then lean over, reaching around to rub her clit. My pace gets faster and harder when I feel my balls tighten. I'm going to come at any moment and I want her to come with me.

Suddenly, the door opens, and my sister walks in with a bag in her hands.

I pull out of Katya quickly and look around for something to cover us, but there's nothing. "What the hell are you doing?" I yell.

Stasya drops the bag and covers her eyes. "Oh my god, Vanya!"

Katya scrambles to cover herself. "I thought Stasya lived somewhere else!" she hisses.

"She does. She—"

My sister doesn't say another word, she just opens the door and exits.

Katya and I meet each other's gaze—and burst out laughing. She sits back on the couch and covers her face with her hands. I lean into her, kissing her neck as we laugh.

"Well, that's one way to ruin the mood," she says, leaning into the cushions.

"Ruin the mood?" I stand and look down at my still fully-erect penis. "My mood is not ruined."

"You're so bad," she teases, reaching up to take my cock in her hands.

My stomach tightens in anticipation as I wait for her to take me into her mouth. "In the best way, yes?"

"You must promise me that it will always be like this."

I glance at her. "Well, it needs about ten minutes between, but—"

"Us, Vanya." She cuts me off and looks into my eyes. "Promise me we'll always forgive and have fun and laugh and make love."

I drop to my knees and wrap my arms around her. "That I can promise, my love."

If I've learned anything in my life, it's that nothing worth having comes easy. Among the good, there will always be pain and tough times woven through. But when it's worth it, you adapt, forgive, and fight. And that's exactly what I plan on doing to keep us together.

THE END

The ice is on fire in this super-sexy short story from USA Today Bestselling Author Sophia Henry's Aviators Hockey series.

Viktor

I didn't realize Lexie Graham, bartender from my favorite local dive, would be working the Jingle Ball, Detroit's most anticipated event of the year. My father wouldn't consider her marriage material, which is fine because I'm looking for a fling, not a ring. The moment I catch her eye from across the room, her bright smile falters for a second and she swallows hard. That's when I know I'll have Lexie in my bed tonight.

* * *

Lexie

Tomorrow, I'll blame it on the stress of being short-staffed or the holiday music that got me feeling sentimental. But tonight, I'm throwing caution to the wind. One night with Viktor Kravtsov, hockey's most eligible bachelor, is exactly what I need to blow off some steam before the stress of the holiday kicks in. I'll consider it an early Christmas present to myself.

Fans of super sexy Russian hockey players with daddy issues, smart-mouth, independent women, and quick romps in casino closets will love Jingle Ball Bender.

Read this steamy short story from *USA Today* Bestselling Author Sophia Henry's Aviators Hockey series. Jingle Ball Bender was originally published in the Jingle Balls Holiday Anthology. *Story is republished with changes.

Turn the Page to start reading
JINGLE BALL BENDER Now!

JINGLE BALL BENDER EXCERPT

AN AVIATORS HOCKEY SHORT STORY

※※

The Commons Family
would be honored by your presence at the Inaugural Motor City
Jingle Ball
to benefit the Testicular Cancer Awareness Foundation

※※

Saturday, December 5th
8pm - Midnight

MoTown Casino Hotel
Detroit, MI

※※

Cocktail hour, gourmet dinner, inspiring onstage program, and silent auction.

The night continues into SoundWaves with dancing, drinks, and late-night snacks.

※※

Black Tie Attire Required

※※

* * *

CHAPTER 1

VIKTOR

Evidently, the Jingle Ball is the most anticipated fundraising gala of the year in Charlotte, North Carolina. I've never been invited to that one, but as someone who's been to my share of extravagant parties over the years, I'm interested to see how the event runs in Detroit. Though, a fundraiser gala is a fundraiser gala, I guess.

Harris and Cookie Commons, who host the ball, own Commons, one of the largest—and fastest growing—Department store chains in the country. A few years ago, they brought the store to Michigan, opening up at multiple mall locations in Metro-Detroit.

And even more recently they bought their second hockey team—the Detroit Aviators, minor league affiliate to the Charlotte Monarchs, the team they own in their hometown.

Since the South isn't really known for hockey—and they don't have any sons who play the sport—I've always wondered how they got the bug up their ass to buy teams.

Evidently, the Commons are going for a big splash in their most Northern location. In addition to bringing the stores and buying a team, they decided to expand their holiday fundraiser and hold an event here, too.

They invited the entire Aviators organization to their annual holiday fundraiser—which is the only reason I got a spot.

I've been to the MoTown Casino a few times, but I've never been in one of the ballrooms. Everything is elegant and high class, enveloping you with luxury from the moment you walk in.

I really hope I get called up to the Monarchs soon. It's not that I mind playing for the Aviators. The organization is top-notch and the fans are amazing. But if I have to stay in this depressing hellhole of a city for much longer, I might beg for a trade.

Spending the first sixteen years of my life here was enough for me.

It's only about five hours away, but when I left home to play for Peterborough in the OHL, it was the happiest day of my life.

Until I was drafted by the Monarchs, that is.

"Hey," Tyler Campbell, one of my teammates, nudges me with his elbow, nodding toward the enormous bar in the corner of the room. "Isn't that the girl from the Beaver?"

I swivel my head. Sure enough, Lexie, the bartender at The Flying Beaver, a local dive we descend on after games, stands behind the bar filling empty flutes with champagne.

The Beaver is one of those amazing hole-in-the wall places that's so laid back, you feel like you're at home. Though we are the NHL stars of the future, minor-league hockey players aren't much of a draw for the city that's home to the Red Wings. It's fairly easy to go unnoticed most places and if anyone does recognize us, they're respectful enough to give us space.

The first time the boys took me to the Beaver was last season after I scored my first goal with the Aviators. While I definitely remember the goal, I have almost no recollection of the celebration.

It must have been a combination of things: lack of a proper meal, dehydration, and drinking a shit-ton of vodka after the game with my cousin (and teammate), Nikolai—Kolya—Antonov. That's all I can think of, because there really wasn't a reason to get blackout drunk. It's not like it was my first goal ever.

That night was one of the few times I've been completely out of control in my life. My father would not be happy. But what he doesn't know won't hurt him.

Lexie glides the tray off the bar carefully and enters the crowd. She looks completely different than I've ever seen her, but still gorgeous. Normally, she's wearing a tight gray T-shirt, cut-off jean shorts, and scuffed cowboy boots with her curly, blonde hair loose and wild. But tonight, her gorgeous hair is pulled back into a sleek ponytail. With the curls tamed and the monotone uniform—a black, button-down dress shirt and matching pants that hug her ass and thighs—she looks almost stern.

All the other servers are women dressed in a sexy version of a Santa suit. I wonder if she wishes she were gliding around in a full, red miniskirt with fluffy white trim or if she thinks she dodged a bullet on that one.

Every detail of the ballroom drips with luxury and class. Which is why I'm honestly surprised the Commons allowed something so tacky as the Santa servers. It doesn't fit with the high-end location and theme of the party.

Lexie stops next to a small crowd of guests, greeting them and offering champagne with a radiant smile and a sparkle in her light eyes. When a blue-hair who has to be triple her age slides her cash, she thanks him, then tucks it into her pocket with a wink.

She looks out into the crowd, and our eyes meet. Her bright smile falters for a second and she swallows before walking toward us.

Pride pumps through my veins. Though I enjoy making her tense up with lust, I'd rather have my face between her legs making her scream.

"Well, well, well. Look at you guys all gussied up," she greets us, balancing the tray of drinks like a pro.

"We could say the same for you," Luke Daniels answers.

Luke is the Director of Player Development for the Charlotte Monarchs, our NHL affiliate. Before he got called up, he was the Captain of the Aviators. After a devastating injury early into his pro career, he had to retire early.

Thankfully, the Monarchs offered him a position in the organization because he's a huge help to us younger guys. Being able to ask his advice about something before getting railed by Coach Vincent has been a blessing.

While all the other guys nod or raise their hands in a wave, I reach out and tuck a chunk of loose hair behind her ear. It's unacceptable for her to look so disheveled at an event like this.

Her eyes widen in surprise, but I shrug it off. "Your hair is a mess."

"Um, thanks, Viktor." She dismisses me with a frown and side-eye as if I've offended her. "I'll have to run to the ladies' room and pin it back when I get a minute. Mr. C doesn't like loose hair hanging all over." She waves a hand around her head as if we need a reminder of how big her hair is. "But mine can be a little unruly sometimes."

The sexy, unruly hair that matches her personality—wild, free, and untamable. A challenge that makes my mouth water and my dick swell.

"Such a double standard," Blake Panikos shakes his head. "He doesn't care if we have flow."

The boys laugh, but Lexie looks confused.

"Flow?" she asks.

"Hair hanging out the back of our helmets." I brush the back of my neck. "Flowing out, if you will."

"Ah, I see." She nods in understanding. "Interesting since he's a very proper man. I'm surprised he lets you have flow or facial hair at all. I can see him running a tight ship."

"Actually, he tried to put a style code in place with the Monarchs, but he nixed it quickly," Luke says. "He finally realized we'd have a harder time attracting top talent if there were such harsh restrictions."

"Well, it's true." I shrug.

Lexie glances to her side, where Harris Commons gathers with a group of people near us. "You guys should probably take a glass, so it looks like I'm working and not having a conversation about the man who signs all of our paychecks."

"Yeah."

"Of course."

"Absolutely."

We each grab a flute of bubbly, emptying her tray.

"Where are your better halves?" Lexie asks, glancing around the room looking for wives and girlfriends. "Did I catch you guys during a group trip to the ladies' room?"

Luke laughs. "No. My wife is helping with the silent auction."

"And none of you guys brought a plus one?" Lexie asks, scanning the group. "How about you, Viktor? Where's your date?"

"Didn't bring one. Wanted to be single in case I ran into a beautiful bartender." I raise an eyebrow and smile.

She swallows thickly and blinks once, then plasters on a smile and shakes the empty tray. "As much as I'd love to stay and shoot the shit with you boys, we can do this at the Beaver because I've gotta get back to work."

When she turns to go, she bumps my shoulder and the tray falls to the floor. We both stoop to get it immediately, slamming heads on our way down.

"Sorry! Sorry!" she says, grimacing as she stands up.

I grab the tray and get back to my feet. "Here you go." When I hand it to her, our eyes lock. That's the moment I know Lexie and I are definitely hooking up tonight. She might not realize it, but I do.

She accepts it, saying, "Thanks. Thank you. I gotta, you know—" She tilts her head to the corner.

"Go pin that wild hair," I call out as she walks away. She looks over her shoulder, pressing her hand to her head as she dashes back to the bar.

"Smooth, Kravtsov. Real smooth." Luke gives me a double-thumbs up.

"You have no game. Like, zero," Blake shakes his head.

No game? What the hell is he talking about? I ooze game. I'm game personified. In the urban dictionary, there's a photo of me next to the definition of game.

"And what's with the creepy shit?" Tyler asks.

"What? What was creepy?" What the hell had I done that these guys think is so wrong?

"Tucking her hair behind her ear." He reaches out with exaggerated slowness, looking at me with half-closed eyes as if he's in a dreamy haze, before mocking how I fixed Lexie's hair. I bat his hand away.

He laughs. "That's a boyfriend move, man."

"No. No. No. You guys are interpreting it wrong!" Kolya waves his hand. "It wasn't a tender move. He was trying to be dominant," he explains, then looks at me pointedly. "Surprised you didn't pee on her."

"That's a territorial thing, not a dominance thing." I correct, brushing off the comment with an eye roll. "Maybe it seemed intimate, but she needs to keep her hair tame at an event like this. I was just trying to help."

Sometimes I don't think before I act. I had an overwhelming urge to touch her—so I did.

Luke agrees. "Tyler's right. It looked very rom-com."

"Whatever." I shrug off their teasing and down my drink. "I gotta hit the head."

On my way to the restroom, I set the empty glass on a small table along the wall of the ballroom.

Unlike some of the other guys, who are constantly tugging at the tightness at their collars, I feel completely at ease at lavish parties like this.

My family owns The Russian Dining Room, a historic restaurant in New York City. We spent many evenings celebrating well into the night. Russian celebrations can last for days. Though, I'm not sure if that's normal or just us. Either way, we know how to party and it's always done with elegance. That—I know—is one of the special things about my family.

My father made international headlines when he defected to Detroit from the former Soviet Union to play hockey. Ivan Kravtsov was the first player from the USSR's Central Scarlet Army to leave without permission.

He doesn't like to talk about it. And though I've been able to pry *some* details out of him, most of what I know about it is from articles on the internet. It was well-documented for the time since it was major historical news.

Kolya's parents, Kirill Antonov and Anastasia Antonova, escaped a short time later. Their story, though not documented like my father's, is just as thrilling—maybe even more so.

Mafia, money, murder—the background of how everyone in our family got to America sounds like something straight out of a suspense novel.

They came here to have a better life and to raise their children with opportunities and freedoms they didn't have.

Which brings me back to the lavish parties. They celebrate the difficult choices they made and good fortune that came from those choices at every opportunity. And they raised all of us—my sisters and my cousins—to appreciate every luxury we enjoy here in America.

As I exit the bathroom, I'm fiddling with my cufflink, and accidentally bump into someone. When I look up to apologize, it's Lexie. Her head is down as she smooths her shirt against her trim stomach. Her hair glistens as if she had to wet it to get it to lay flat.

"Sorry," I say, bracing her by placing my hands on her biceps.

"I'm so sorry, sir, I—" she stammers before looking up. Once she sees me, a relieved sigh escapes her lips. "Oh, it's just you."

I lower my arms. "Just me? What does that mean?"

"It means I have more leniency bumping you." She pats my shoulder as if consoling a child before sweeping past me. "No need to get offended, Viktor."

"Someone's going to get hurt if we keep running into each other like this," I call out. "I can think of much better ways to touch each other."

She shakes her head without turning around.

Dropping my original mission to rejoin the guys, I spin around and follow her. The urge to have Lexie in my bed tonight is greater than the urge to listen to Luke rehash last night's game against Philly.

Please, Luke, tell us again how we need to capitalize on the Power Play.

She must know I'm a step behind because I catch her looking at me out of the corner of her eye. But she doesn't stop or glance back.

I love a challenge. It's been awhile since I used my primal impulse to hunt.

"Are you lost?" she asks, as she rounds the corner of a long bar. She grabs a ticket printing from the machine behind her and scans it before scooping ice into a stainless-steel tumbler, then adding vodka and cranberry juice.

"Yes. Lost in thoughts of you." I place an elbow on the bar and lean toward her.

"Oh my gosh!" She rolls her eyes while screwing the cap on the vodka bottle. "Does that line ever work?"

"It's true. I can't get you out of my head, Lexie. I've been thinking about you since the first time we met. You realize that by now, right?"

"Really?" Her lips curve into a playful smile as she shakes the liquids and ice in a stainless-steel tumbler. "I didn't realize you had any recollection of the night we met."

"Well." I scratch the back of my neck while twisting my lips. "I mean, I think I do."

Her eyes narrow slightly, toying with me. "You remember the night you got to the Beaver already so drunk that I wouldn't serve you *and* I had to pay for your ride home?"

Her words spark a memory, but not everything comes back to me. I rub the back of my neck and laugh. "I wondered how I got to my apartment."

"You didn't know how you got home?" She lifts her gaze to mine quickly while straining the drink into two frosted martini glasses.

"Nope." I chuckle. I always thought one of the boys took me home. Never even questioned it. "Sounds like I owe you a ride."

We both pause, realizing the sexual double entendre in my comment. Her cheeks heat up with a rosy tone as her gaze burns into me, lust seeping out like molten lava. She wants me just as much as I want her.

The question isn't *if* we'll have sex, but *when*.

"Come on! You've got to let me repay you. How about tonight?" I persist.

"No, thanks." Just then, a server reaches over me and grabs the drinks she just finished preparing while Lexie tends to the machine that keeps spewing paper. "Not trying to be a jerk, but"—she nods to the printer—"I'm kinda busy here."

"You're working, I get it." I tap my hand on the bar. "I'll have a vodka neat."

KEEP READING

REVIEWS ROCK!

THANK YOU so much for taking the time to read **EVEN STRENGTH!**

I truly appreciate every single one of you.

If you enjoyed reading **EVEN STRENGTH** as much as I enjoyed writing it, it would mean the world to me if you would consider leaving a review on Amazon.

DON'T MISS OUT!

Sophia Henry's mailing list is the place to be if you like steamy romance novels that tug at your heart strings. Stay notified of new releases, sales, exclusive content with newsletters twice a month. Get a FREE book when you sign up at sophiahenry.com.

* * *

Join Sophia's Reader Group

When you join Sophia's Patreon Community you get exclusive access to AUDIO of her books, get sneak peeks, exclusive posts, and extra surprises just for members. You even get to name characters! (Seriously, it happens. Sophia's readers named Zayne, the hero of CRAZY FOR YOU).

Join the Fun: patreon.com/sophiahenry313

* * *

Merch Store

ALSO BY SOPHIA HENRY

SAINTS AND SINNERS SERIES

Ebook and Paperback Available on Amazon

SAINTS

SINNERS

AVIATORS HOCKEY SERIES

Ebook and Paperback Available on Amazon

DELAYED PENALTY

POWER PLAY

UNSPORTSMANLIKE CONDUCT

JINGLE BALL BENDER: An Aviators Hockey Short Story

BLUE LINES

STANDALONE CROSSOVER NOVELS

EVEN STRENGTH

Saints & Sinners/Aviators Hockey Crossover Novel

DEVIL IN DISGUISE

Material Girls/Saints & Sinners Crossover Novel

MATERIAL GIRLS SERIES

Ebook and Paperback Available on Amazon

OPEN YOUR HEART

LIVE TO TELL

CRAZY FOR YOU

* * *

FOREIGN EDITIONS

FRENCH

SAGA MATERIAL GIRLS

OPEN YOUR HEART

LIVE TO TELL

CRAZY FOR YOU

DEVIL IN DISGUISE

DUO SAINTS AND SINNERS

SAINTS

SINNERS

ROMANS AUTONOMES LIÉS AUX SAGAS

EVEN STRENGTH

Saints & Sinners/Aviators Hockey Crossover Novel

SAGA AVIATORS HOCKEY

JINGLE BALL BENDER

BLUE LINES

* * *

GERMAN

MATERIAL GIRLS SERIES

OPEN YOUR HEART

LIVE TO TELL

CRAZY FOR YOU

* * *

RUSSIAN

SAINTS AND SINNERS DUET

SAINTS

SINNERS

ABOUT THE AUTHOR

USA Today Bestselling Author Sophia Henry is a proud Detroit native who fell in love with reading, writing, and hockey all before she became a teenager. After graduating with a Creative Writing degree from Central Michigan University, she moved to warm and sunny North Carolina where she spent twenty glorious years before heading back to her roots and settling in Michigan.

She spends her days writing steamy, heartfelt contemporary romance and posting personal stories in her Patreon community hoping they resonate with and encourage others. When Sophia's not writing, she's hanging out with her two high-energy sons, an equally high-energy Plott Hound, and two cats who want nothing to do with any of them. She can also be found watching her beloved Detroit Red Wings and rocking out at as many concerts as she can possibly attend.

Receive a FREE ebook and get all the latest releases and updates exclusively for readers! Subscribe to Sophia's newsletter today. https://bit.ly/FreeSHBookNL